ALSO BY GARTH NIX

Newt's Emerald

GARTH NIX

KT KATHERINE TEGEN BOOKS
An Imprint of HarperCollins Publishers

Katherine Tegen Books is an imprint of HarperCollins Publishers.

Newt's Emerald
Copyright © 2015 by Garth Nix
All rights reserved. Printed in the United States of America.
No part of this book may be used or reproduced in any manner whatsoever
without written permission except in the case of brief quotations embodied in critical
articles and reviews. For information address HarperCollins Children's Books,
a division of HarperCollins Publishers, 195 Broadway, New York, NY 10007.
www.epicreads.com

Library of Congress Cataloging-in-Publication Data
Nix, Garth.
Newt's emerald / Garth Nix.
pages   cm
"Previously published in a somewhat different format in 2013."
Summary: After the Newington Emerald is stolen at the height of a conjured storm,
eighteen-year-old Lady Truthful Newington goes to London, disguised as a man, to
search for the magical heirloom of her house, and is soon caught up in a dangerous
adventure where she must risk her life, her reputation, and her heart.
ISBN 978-0-06-236004-5 (hardcover)
[1. Adventure and adventurers—Fiction.   2. Magic—Fiction.
3. Sex role—Fiction.   4. Love—Fiction.   5. London—History—19th century—
Fiction.   6. Great Britain—History—George III, 1760–1820—Fiction.]   I. Title.
PZ7.N647New 2015   2014041258
[Fic]—dc23   CIP   AC

Typography by Carla Weise
15 16 17 18 19   PC/RRDH   10 9 8 7 6 5 4 3 2 1

First Edition

TO MY FAMILY AND FRIENDS

LADY TRUTHFUL'S BIRTHDAY

Of all the birthdays she'd had, Truthful decided her present one was the best and most exciting. It seemed very fine to be eighteen years old and to finally be on the brink of being launched into fashionable society in London. Not that she was dissatisfied with Newington Hall and its beautiful gardens and lawns that sloped down to the widely envied cliff walk bordering the vast perspective of the English Channel. Nor was she in any way exasperated by living with her sole surviving parent, Admiral the Viscount Newington, even though she might well have been since he had come late to fatherhood, was past sixty, and was inclined to be curmudgeonly when he suffered from the gout.

Truthful also never tired of the company of her neighbors and cousins. Edmund, Stephen, and Robert Newington-Lacy had always been like brothers to her and Truthful had spent nearly every summer of her life with them, when they returned from Harrow and she could escape her tutors.

But she had to admit that she would *quite* like to see something of the wider world, so to be eighteen and on the very threshold of a triumphal entry (or at least a credible arrival) into the fashionable London *ton* was both very satisfactory and exciting, though Truthful had to admit to herself that she was almost as much frightened as thrilled.

This was particularly so because in her own mind Truthful was not at all sure she would make even a credible debut, despite what everyone told her. Others saw a lithe and fresh-faced beauty with green eyes and gorgeously thick hair of the deepest russet hue. But when Truthful looked in a mirror she mostly noticed remnant signs of the freckles that had until recently spread themselves generously over her nose and cheeks. She feared her beauty was a purely local phenomenon, the result of a scarcity of young ladies of quality.

In London, Truthful felt sure she would be considered plain, particularly as her sorcerous talents did not include any particular skill with the glamours that would enhance her charms. Truthful had the small weather magic that ran in her family; she could raise a gentle breeze, or soothe a drizzle. In addition to this, horses and other animals liked her and would do her bidding. But she had none of the greater arts, and little formal training.

But plain or not, magically gifted or not, she must make the best of it, she decided. And it was her birthday, so she soon forgot about her freckles and threw herself into the preparations for her small party, giving her maid, Agatha, a sore trial in her dressing, as she would try on all three new gowns sent down from town by her great-aunt Ermintrude.

"This one, I think," she cried to Agatha, pirouetting in a dress of deep green satin that was rather shockingly low cut in the bodice and had transparent sleeves of a fine lace. At least, Truthful felt it was shocking, but her great-aunt had in fact selected the dresses to be considerably more demure than the latest fashion. Truthful would have been shocked to see some of those dresses, and what some of the faster female set could do with strategically dampened muslin. Not to mention the most daring, who would use a glamour to wreathe a plain under-dress in what looked like gorgeous satins and crapes, sure to dissolve at the touch of a gentleman's silver watch chain or signet ring.

Truthful pirouetted again, causing a shower of pins to fall from Agatha's hand.

"Oh, Agatha, I am sorry!"

Agatha scowled and bent to pick them up. Truthful tried to bend down to help her, but the dress was really rather tight above the waist, so she said, "I think I am a little, just a little . . . excited today."

"Mmmmf," muttered Agatha, who was holding several pins in her mouth. The pins were old and hints of bronze were showing through worn tin plating, which, to someone with an arcane education, would indicate Agatha could not touch iron, that there was fay blood in the older woman.

Truthful had not had such an education. She had never noticed Agatha's particular pins or how the maid would wrap her hand in her apron to turn a key, should it prove absolutely necessary. If she had, it might not have alarmed her. Even some of the higher nobility had fay blood from the distant past, and not all the old fairy folk were by nature inimical to humans.

Agatha took the pins from her mouth and said, "What's to be excited about, my lady?"

"Why, Agatha!" laughed Truthful. "It's my birthday, you silly goose. And Papa is going to show the Newington Emerald to all my friends."

"The Emerald?" asked Agatha. "Shown to all your friends? You mean those Lacy boys?"

4

"They're Newington-Lacys, Agatha," replied Truthful. "And they are young men, not boys."

"Aye. And no good will come of mixing young men and emeralds, you mark my words," grumbled Agatha. She put the pins back in her mouth and her face resumed its customary scowl.

"I'm sorry I made you spill your pins," said Truthful. "But it is my birthday, and it is exciting! Oh, I can hear a carriage in the drive. They must be here already—I have to go down!"

Agatha mumbled and nodded, and tacked the last inch of the hem in place. With a parting cry of thanks, Truthful fairly leaped from the room, leaving Agatha searching for any pins that might have rolled away.

Downstairs, the three Newington-Lacy boys were making their bows to the Admiral, who had launched himself from his study and bore down to meet them, propelled by a good humor that had been reinforced by the excellent claret he'd broached on the excuse of tasting it before Truthful's birthday dinner.

Truthful paused on the stairs, hoping to achieve the awed silence inspired by all heroines as they stood framed in sunlight on the middle landing. But, as she had misjudged the light and stopped in shadow, no one noticed her.

Not a bit put off, she paused to look at the men in her life instead.

The Admiral, as her father, came first under her gaze. Admiral the Viscount Newington had been a senior post captain under Nelson, fighting under that great commander at Aboukir, Copenhagen, and Trafalgar. At the last battle, he had been wounded in the leg, and although he survived to continue seagoing service for a decade (rising to the rank of Rear-Admiral of the Blue) it marked the beginning of the gout that sorely plagued him and the drinking with which he exacerbated his affliction.

He had been retired for several years now, and Truthful had found the distant, none-too-frequent visitor of her childhood to be a loving, if somewhat difficult, father, when he finally came to harbor at the ancestral home.

Truthful had never really known her mother. A renowned glamouress and a granddaughter of the famous sorcerer Marquis of Perraworth, Venetia Newington had died when Truthful was six. She had only fleeting memories of her mother, disconnected moments: a song, sung softly in dim light over her bed; laughter and cold, throwing snowballs together on the slope of Old Hill behind the house; a soft finger drawn under her eyes to wipe away tears . . .

Looking at the red-flushed, roly-poly face of her father, she wondered how such a paragon of beauty and magic as her mother had fallen in love with a considerably older, irascible Naval officer whose prospects were as slight as his personal attractions, two older brothers standing between him and the Fifth Viscount's coronet. But it had been a love match, according to her great-aunt Ermintrude, and the coronet had soon followed the wedding, when both elder brothers had died in somewhat mysterious circumstances while the youngest was away at sea.

Love was passing strange, mused Truthful as she transferred her gaze from her father to the Newington-Lacys. They had been her friends since her earliest childhood, and up until the past few years she spent much of her time with them, often disguised as a boy so she could share in pursuits that were deemed unfitting for a girl, such as horse racing or watching a mill, as they called a boxing match. She still missed those outings, though she doubted she could pass for a young man now. At least not without a glamour.

Edmund Newington-Lacy, the eldest of the three, was a fingerbreadth above six feet in height, dark haired and brown eyed, and had a very martial carriage. His character was one of seriousness, and he applied this single-mindedly to everything he did. He had come down from Oxford with an undistinguished degree and was soon to go into the Army, doubtless the beginning of a glorious career. His paternal uncle was a colonel at the Horse Guards, and his father was deep enough in the pocket to purchase both Edmund's initial commission and as many promotions as he might need. If he possessed any magical talent, it was small, and he did not display it.

Stephen Newington-Lacy was next. He looked up as she gazed down, and Truthful smiled at the twinkle in his green eyes. It was typical that he would feel her glance, for he was the most eldritch of the three, with strange quirks of knowledge and stranger interests. He talked without words to birds and animals, and often knew what Truthful or his brothers were thinking.

Stephen did not have the Lacy looks. He took after the Newington side of the family, and in fact much resembled Truthful. In addition to the green eyes he also had deep red hair, was of a slight build, and was the same height as his cousin. This may have induced him to attempt the growing of a moustache in recent months, his brothers having often teased him that he could put on a dress and exchange places with Truthful without any particular notice. He had just gone up to Cambridge, and would likely stay there as an academic sorcerer.

Standing behind his brothers, but looming over both of them, was Robert. He was a Lacy on a larger scale. Not only was he very tall, he was also broad, his light hair framing a rounder face than his brothers'. As Truthful looked, he burst into laughter at something the Admiral said, and soon all four were guffawing, infected with Robert's sense of the absurd.

He was in many ways an unusual son for a country peer, for he had a fondness for machines and devices. Robert would always take steam engines over horses, and iron foundries over hounds. His magical talents were complementary, for he was a ferromancer, who could work iron with sorcery as well as tools.

Robert was in his last year at Harrow, and his future was a sore point with his parents, who refused to countenance his desire to be an inventor and engineer. A real engineer, not just an idle dabbler, utilizing both his mathematical mind and his ferromantic talents to design, build, and operate new mechanisms and devices. But Truthful knew that Robert would end up doing what he really wanted, with a laugh and a wink at his parents that would overcome their distaste for his chosen profession.

Truthful sighed as she once again confirmed that she loved them all equally. As brothers. Being careful to take suitably ladylike steps in her new silver slippers, she proceeded down the stairs to greet them properly.

"Ah, Truthful, my dear, you have come down," exclaimed the Admiral.

Truthful smiled at him and held out her hand to the

Newington-Lacys, who queued in order of age to gently hold her fingers, kiss her lightly on the cheek, and wish her happy birthday.

That courtesy taken care of, the Admiral inquired after Sir Reginald Newington-Lacy and his wife, who were visiting the shrine of Saint Ethburga and taking the waters at Bath. It was hoped this would cure Lady Angela's weariness, which had progressed beyond a fashionable ennui to a state quite alarming to her family.

"Father says that the statue of Saint Ethburga moved two fingers in a blessing, and the waters are also having a beneficial effect," replied Edmund. "They fully expect to be home within a sennight."

"Oh, I do hope Aunt Angela is quite recovered," said Truthful. "They say the waters at Bath are very invigorating. I should like to go to Bath myself, though perhaps . . . perhaps not to the shrine of Saint Ethburga. I've always thought it sounds rather frightening."

"Better off at the shrine than wandering about Bath with all those young bucks that promenade there," grunted the Admiral. "Bah! Half the fellows are damn man-milliners! Shirt points up to their cheeks, cut their ears if they turn sideways, and damn me if they don't festoon themselves with charms and gewgaws!"

He glared at the Newington-Lacys, as if amulet fobs and

spell-breaking watch chains were about to sprout from their waistcoats, despite the fact that they were all rather soberly attired in blue long-tailed coats, starched linen shirts without excessively high collars, fawn waistcoats, knee breeches, and black slippers. Only Edmund went so far as to sport his neckcloth in a style more daring than a simple triangular tie, and even he only dared the Osbaldeston. They were, in short, fittingly attired as country gentlemen come to dinner.

"I should like to go to all the balls and assemblies," replied Truthful. She had been to small provincial assemblies in Canterbury, but of course Bath had far superior offerings without being quite so frightening as London.

"Hmmmph," interrupted the Admiral. "You'll get enough of that in London with your great-aunt, puss. Only a few weeks till you go. I shall miss you, but your mother would never forgive me if I kept you mewed up here to keep an old salt like me company. Let's go in to dinner."

There were only the five of them for the meal, for the Admiral was not fond of society, or any neighbors save the Newington-Lacys. Truthful played her role as hostess from one end of the table, and the Admiral that of host from the other.

Turbot with lobster sauce, several boiled fowls, a turtle, a ham, and a quarter of a lamb with cauliflowers adorned the table in rapid succession, followed by a gooseberry and currant pie, a soft pudding, and five different sorts of fruit, all washed down with the Admiral's champagne, Burgundy, and Madeira, though Truthful surreptitiously drank lemonade in her champagne glass, with the knowing cooperation of the servants.

Everyone ate heartily, the young men gently chaffing the Admiral to tell tales of his Naval exploits. He needed little encouragement and proceeded to do so at some length, stressing his advice to Nelson at Trafalgar (neglecting to mention he was actually on a different ship), and the importance of "cutting the line."

Then he turned from tales of war at sea to tales of storm and shipwreck. He had barely moved on from describing some common storms to the story of a hurricane off Jamaica when the air began to cool and the sound of distant thunder could be heard like the far-off guns in the Admiral's tale of Trafalgar.

"Why, bless me!" he cried. Like many Naval officers, he was a weather-wizard, and had grown too enthusiastic in his storytelling, investing power in his words. "Here I am talking up a storm, and there it is! Truthful, please ring the bell for Hetherington. We must secure the place for a gale."

"Batten the hatches?" asked Stephen, smiling.

The Admiral, his good humor further sustained by an

excellent dinner, laughed and said, "Just so, my boy. Hetherington! Ah, there you are. We are about to have a storm upon us, and the shutters aren't on! Have them brought to and fastened, and make sure James is with the horses. You know what to do."

Hetherington almost brought his fist to his head to salute before remembering to bow instead. He had been the Admiral's coxswain, and still found it difficult to play the butler rather than the petty officer he had been for twenty years. Retreating, his stentorian voice could be heard above the approaching storm, directing the footmen and maids to their tasks.

"Now, my dear," said the Admiral jovially. "A storm is a good time to show your heirloom and its powers. A little advance glimpse of the stone that shall be yours when you turn twenty-one."

"Twenty-one!" exclaimed Truthful. "I thought I wouldn't inherit the Emerald till I am twenty-five."

"Twenty-one, twenty-five, what does it matter?" cried the Admiral impatiently. "I can never remember the details. Your mother wore it so seldom, you see. Unlike my mother, who wore it on every possible occasion, and used it, too."

He turned to look at the portrait above the fireplace behind him, which portrayed a stern-looking woman backed by dense storm clouds.

"That's her there, lads. Truthful's grandmama, Héloise Newington, wearing the Emerald."

"May I?" asked Edmund, indicating that he wished to look closer. The Admiral nodded and Edmund got up, took one of the candelabra from the table, and raised it to the portrait.

The sudden light falling on the painting made two things leap out at the watchers: Héloise's green eyes, and the glowing emerald that hung on a silver chain about her neck.

"Why," said Edmund, "she has beautiful eyes. More beautiful than any gem."

"She broke many hearts before my father caught hers," chuckled the Admiral. "Though some say it was the Emerald that caught her, not Father."

"Oh, no!" exclaimed Truthful. "Surely not!"

"No, my dear," said the Admiral. "She loved the Emerald well, but it was not the stone that sealed the marriage."

"It must be a remarkable gem," said Stephen, who had gotten up to examine the portrait as well. "It is cut in an Oriental fashion, if I'm any judge."

"Though what Stephen knows about such matters you could inscribe on the head of a pin," remarked Robert, smiling to show he wasn't serious.

"On the contrary, dear brother," replied Stephen. "I have recently read a most learned monograph on the subject of the cutting and ensorcellment of gems, and have also in fact visited Messrs. Longhurst and Everett in London to see just such an operation."

"Well, perhaps the head of a very large pin . . ." said Robert, gesturing with his arms to indicate a very large pin indeed.

"I didn't know you were so interested in the subject," said Edmund, turning from the portrait in surprise. "But then, it is no stranger than any other subject you have pursued."

"And much more salubrious than the sorcerous enlargement of frogs," added Robert, causing everyone to laugh except Stephen, who exclaimed that it was very important work and that huge anuran steeds might one day serve as amphibious cavalry.

"Enough of this talk of frogs!" interrupted the Admiral to quell the laughter. "It's Truthful's birthday, and she must see the Emerald. Please wait here."

With a grunt of exertion, he levered himself out of his chair and crossed to a small and discreet door in the wooden panelling of the south wall. Opening it with a tiny key shot from a ring on his forefinger, he stepped within.

As he did so, lightning flashed outside, followed by thunder and the sudden din of rain. All around the house, those shutters still unfastened began to bang against the window frames. Another bolt of lightning struck, and everyone blinked. When they opened their eyes, the Admiral had closed the little door behind him.

"I always thought that was a cupboard," said Robert. "It can't open into the hall or into your parlor, Truthful."

"No, it doesn't," said Truthful. "I've never really thought about it. Papa rarely opens it, and I presumed it was a pantry to store his more precious port."

The storm sounded again as the small door reopened, and the Admiral's emerging face was lit with a flash of lightning, closely followed by a resounding clap of thunder.

"By Jove, the storm's closing fast. Bigger than I thought, too strong to quell now!" exclaimed the admiral. "That last levinbolt damme near got the house, and the shutters still ain't up!"

He crossed to the windows and looked out into the heavy rain, much as he must have gazed from the heaving quarterdeck of a ship of the line.

"Where is Hetherington?" the Admiral asked peevishly, but before anyone could answer, his question was dramatically answered. The lightning flashed again, revealing an oilskin-clad Hetherington and several sodden footmen struggling up to the windows with a wheelbarrow stacked high with shutters.

"I didn't realize you'd had the shutters taken right off," said Stephen. "Why on earth—"

"Oh, Father likes to have them repainted at least twice a year, each room in turn. So they have to come off," interrupted Truthful hastily, with a warning glance to Stephen. "They've been drying in the coach house."

"Namby-pamby things anyway," said the Admiral, waving to Hetherington to hurry up as two of the men struggled to fit the first shutter on its heavy iron hinges. "Wouldn't put them up at all if it weren't for the womenfolk. A few shards of glass never did anyone any lasting harm. I like to feel a good storm. Why, I remember off Cape Finisterre in '08, I was in *Defiant*, and—"

"Sir, you were going to show us the Emerald," interrupted Stephen, earning him a stern glance from Edmund.

"Why, of course," replied the Admiral, as if he'd suddenly thought of it himself. "I've got it right here."

He lumbered back to his chair and gently lowered himself into it. Once secure, he felt in the pockets of his waistcoat, first the left, then the right. A look of consternation began to spread across his face, to be rapidly mirrored in the others, as he gave every appearance of a man who has somehow managed to lose something extraordinarily precious!

2

THE SHOWING OF THE EMERALD

Then the Admiral laughed and pulled a package from *inside* his waistcoat.

"Thought I'd slipped my moorings, didn't you?" he chuckled, pushing the bag over to Truthful. "Open it, my dear. But don't put it on. You aren't ready to wield it yet. Particularly not in a storm."

Truthful leaned forward eagerly, before deliberately slowing herself. Taking a little half breath, half gasp, she carefully untied the gold drawstring of the small velvet bag. That successfully done, she reached inside, and pulled out . . . the Emerald.

A huge, heart-shaped gem of the clearest green, it hung suspended from a silver necklace of filigreed leaves. The candlelight flickered on the silver, and small green fires danced from the many facets of the stone, hinting at the sorcerous powers that lurked within.

"It's beautiful," said Truthful. "Too beautiful for me. I can't possibly wear it! Not even when I'm twenty-five."

"You will," said the Admiral fondly. "You have your mother's looks, you know. A good thing, too; I'd have disliked it excessively if you'd had mine."

"Oh, Father," cried Truthful. "Don't be silly! It must be far too valuable to wear anyway."

"At least thirty thousand pounds, I would say," said Stephen. He held out his hand, adding, "Merely as a gemstone, without knowing the extent of its sorcerous powers. Is it safe for me to hold?"

"Aye," said the Admiral. "It don't answer unless worn at the neck, and only to the family. The womenfolk. It has never answered to a man, so far as is known."

Truthful reluctantly handed over the gem, the silver leaves trickling through her fingers as the stone dropped into Stephen's palm. Truthful watched its slow fall, dazed at the beauty and size of the gem. Even from the brief moment in her hand she felt an affinity for it, and had to suppress an urge to ask for it back. Privately she was very sure it was far too beautiful for her to own, let alone wear or to attempt to use its powers. Whatever those powers might be. The Admiral had never really talked to her about the Emerald's magic. It was probably something her mother would have told her about, and as with many other such things, the Admiral had simply forgotten.

Stephen looked at the Emerald for several minutes, holding it close to his right eye, even dragging a candle to shine behind the gem.

"There is a great and ancient power in the stone," he said. As so often, he seemed to know what Truthful was thinking and asked her question for her. "What precisely is its nature, and how does it manifest?"

"Precisely never you mind," retorted the Admiral. "Ain't none of your business."

Stephen smiled and passed the stone to Robert.

Robert looked at it, felt the weight, and said, "Sell it at once, and put the money into Mr. Watt's new steam donkeys."

"Don't be silly!" exclaimed Edmund, taking up the gem. "It's an heirloom of the family, and besides must be a restricted item under the terms of the Sorcerous Trading Act. Besides, it will look very handsome indeed on Truthful."

He put the gem down in the center of the table and pushed it a few inches toward Truthful.

"There, back to its rightful place—" he began just as

lightning struck the iron-framed windows.

Light flooded the entire room. Simultaneously, someone outside cried in pain, glass shattered, and thunder clapped. The wind and rain rushed in, quenching the candles and plunging the room into total darkness.

Truthful leaped to her feet, knocking her chair backward. The men shouted, and crashing and splintering noises attested to their efforts to get up, knocking chairs over and sending the table sliding on its castors as they struggled to get free of the debris from the broken windows.

Lightning flashed again, farther away, the instant of light showing wild figures leaping around the table, and the shapes of men grappling together outside. Then all was dark again, and thunder resounded through the room, quickly followed by the bull-roar of the Admiral's seagoing voice of command, infused with the full strength of his native sorcery.

"Be still!"

Quiet came after his shout, the elements also bound by his command. The lightning and thunder retreated, the storm rolling out across the cliffs toward the sea. A few seconds later, a dull roar rumbled in as its departing cry. At the same time, the double doors opened, revealing Agatha holding a storm lantern, its wick turned high. Behind her stood one of the kitchen maids with a fire bucket full of sand.

The flickering light of the lantern showed a scene of destruction. One of the unfixed shutters had blown clear through the windows, showering both glass and bits of frame throughout the room. Outside, Hetherington and three footmen slowly let each other go and stood back, scratching their heads.

"There was someone ran past us," said Hetherington, disbelieving. "Come in with the storm, like."

"Aye, like a cloud or smoke," said a footman. "I thought I had 'im, but it was Jukes here."

"I thought you *was* him," said Jukes.

"Sorcery," said Stephen. "Perhaps a natural adjunct of the storm . . . or perhaps not."

He and his brothers stood close together by the shifted table. There were glasses and dishes distributed widely among overturned chairs, several of which were smashed beyond repair. Everyone was drenched with rain, and Edmund had a small cut on his forehead, which was slowly bleeding into his right eyebrow.

Truthful looked at the wreckage and held her hands to her face as the shock of the sudden transition from happy party to disaster took hold. In a second, Agatha was at her side, pausing only to thrust the lantern into the maid's hands.

"You sit down, my lady," she said, kneeling to right a

chair, her voluminous skirts billowing up as she crouched down.

"Thank you," said Truthful. She didn't particularly feel the need to sit, but did so obediently until Agatha started to fuss about with her smelling salts.

"I don't need smelling salts, Agatha!" protested Truthful. "I never do faint, you know that. I was momentarily shocked, but all seems to be well."

"Hmmph," said the Admiral, who had stepped through the broken window to investigate the damage to both building and servants. "I don't know about this smoky character you reckon to have seen, Hetherington, but the storm has done its work. A nine-pound ball could do as much, and I've seen a storm do a great deal more. Let's straighten the table, gentlemen. We'll adjourn to the card room. I'll have the builders in tomorrow."

He bent to one corner of the table, and the three brothers distributed themselves accordingly, gingerly picking their way through the debris.

"One—two—three—heave!" cried the Admiral, and the table was slid back in place. He gazed down on its polished surface happily, observed there wasn't a single irreparable scratch, and then his smile faded like a powder dissolving in a glass. A red flush spread up his neck and across his face, and he swayed on his feet as he tried to speak.

"The Emerald! Where is the—"

This was all he got out before he pitched headfirst onto the table, his great bulk making it resound like an enormous drum.

✦ ‒‒‒ ✦

The Admiral lay senseless for two whole days while every inch of the dining room was searched for the Emerald to no avail. Even the floorboards were taken up, but they revealed only several rat right-of-ways, a tinware spoon, and a clipped silver penny of Elizabeth's reign.

On the morning of the third day, the Admiral awoke and called for a hot rum punch, well-spiced with cinnamon. Truthful brought it up herself and was pleased to see his normal color returning as he drank it.

"Thank you, my dear," he said, handing the glass back to her. "A proper cast-up mackerel I must look! I hear those rapscallions have come to visit. Has one of them handed back the Emerald?"

"Rapscallions?" cried Truthful. "Oh, no, Father! You can't mean the Newington-Lacys!"

"You mean to say the Emerald ain't back?" expostulated the Admiral, raising himself angrily up on one elbow. "Yes, I do mean the Newington-Lacys. No one else could have taken it! I don't hold that a smoke-devil or cloud-catcher could have done so, no matter what Hetherington thinks he saw!"

He looked fiercely at Truthful, but his eyes were focused somewhere beyond her shocked face.

"You don't understand, Truthful," continued the Admiral fretfully. "The Emerald isn't just a jewel, not merely some sorcerous piece for working the wind and sea as is commonly believed. It is a great stone of power. We have kept its full potential secret for generations for fear of its theft and misuse. But even more than that, it's the luck of the Newingtons! The last time it went missing, a hundred and twenty years ago, the whole family damn near came to an end. Two brothers killed at Marston Moor, another at Naseby . . . a sister dead of the smallpox . . . all the plate confiscated—"

"But Father, you can't say the rebellion was caused by the loss of the Emerald," interrupted Truthful. She laid her palm across his forehead, hoping to calm him, but he angrily shrugged it off. "Besides, I am quite certain that it has *not* been taken by the Newington-Lacys."

"West wing of the house burned down," continued the Admiral, his eyes rolling back and forth like an unsteady deck. "Before that, when the Emerald was misplaced for a week, Sir Tancred Newington broke both legs. My brother pledged it at play once, died of a fever . . . Emerald. Bad blood in the Lacy family, there was that great-great-uncle of theirs, took to living in a cave and wouldn't eat honest mutton . . ."

"Father!" exclaimed Truthful as the tirade continued unabated, becoming more and more incoherent as the Admiral began to thrash about in the bed despite her efforts to calm him. Finally, she managed to get him to drink a draft of laudanum. As he grew quieter the gaze of reason came back in his eyes.

"Just tell the boys to put it back," he whispered, holding out his bearlike palm. "Put it in my hand."

Truthful put her small gloved hand in his and said, "Yes, Papa."

A second later, the Admiral lapsed back into sleep. Truthful let her hand rest in his for a moment, then withdrew it gently and went downstairs, her head bowed in thought.

The Newington-Lacys were waiting for Truthful in the yellow drawing room, each with a large glass of Hetherington's punch in hand, a half-empty silver bowl on the table indicating that they had been waiting for some time. Truthful darted a glance at the faithful retainer who stood by the bowl, hoping to judge both the strength of the punch and how much Hetherington had himself "tasted" before serving it to the visitors. There was certainly rather a strong aroma of rum in the air, suggesting that the "three parts strong" of the punch recipe might have been overdone. Hetherington himself, as a former Navy man, could put away vast quantities of rum without immediately obvious effect, but the young gentlemen certainly weren't used to such stuff.

"I trust you haven't been waiting long," she said anxiously.

"Not above an hour," said Edmund. He stood up carefully and set his glass down on the table. He didn't seem to be drunk, Truthful noted, but she was a little alarmed at how slowly he was moving. . . .

"Hetherington made us a punch," said Stephen, indicating the bowl.

"A very good punch," said Robert, beaming.

"Oh dear," said Truthful. "I think, Hetherington, you had best bring coffee now. Lots of coffee. And take this punch away!"

"Aye, aye, milady," said Hetherington. But he didn't move. He just stood there blinking, his eyes glassy.

"Oh, he must have drunk at least two bottles," said Truthful with a sigh. She went to the corner and pulled on the bell rope. "You should know you must never let Hetherington make a punch without my father present. He will drink the rum straight."

"Very good punch," said Robert.

"I am sure it is an excellent punch," said Truthful. "But I do wish you had all drunk rather less of it!"

"Not drunk," said Edmund carefully. "A trifle bosky, perhaps."

"We do beg your pardon," said Stephen. "Suspect the punch a trifle stronger than expected."

"Very good punch," said Robert.

A footman appeared at the door, his face professionally blank, though he couldn't help his eyes shifting toward Hetherington.

"Jukes, I'm afraid Hetherington has sampled too much of his . . . mixture," said Truthful. "If you could assist him, and ask Ellen to bring up a large . . . no, several large pots of coffee."

"Yes, milady," said Jukes stolidly. He went to Hetherington's side and took his elbow. "This way, Mr. Hetherington, that's it. One foot after the other."

"How . . . how is the Admiral?" asked Edmund. He was clearly making a tremendous effort to talk.

"Have you found the Emerald?" asked Stephen.

"Very good punch," said Robert.

"Father is extremely unwell," said Truthful, sitting down with a spiritless thump. "And there is no sign of the Emerald."

"Decidedly odd," said Edmund. He blinked several times and added, "Odd."

"It's worse than *odd*," said Truthful. "Father's not quite right in his mind. He thinks losing the Emerald means the end of the Newingtons . . . and he thinks one of you took it."

"What!"

Edmund and Stephen spoke together. Robert smiled at them, apparently not having heard a word.

"Us!" exclaimed Edmund, scandalized. "Us! Steal the Emerald?"

"Yes," said Truthful sadly. "Of course it's silly, but the shock . . ."

"We shall be infamous if this comes out," muttered Edmund. He made as if to slam his fist on the table, but stopped when it was clear his balance wasn't up to it. "Our name blighted!"

"Not as bad as that," said Stephen. "I mean . . . what do I mean? Lord, we need that coffee, Newt! Where was I?"

"I don't know," said Truthful crossly. "I think it is very unhelpful of you all to be so drunk when I need sound advice."

"Not drunk," said Edmund. "Told you. Just a little . . . ah . . ."

"Astray," suggested Stephen. "Ah, I remember! Who will find out? The Admiral won't be receiving, not if he's touched in the rafters, begging your pardon, Truthful. I meant unwell. When he gets better, he won't talk such nonsense."

"Lady Troutbridge is visiting this afternoon," said Truthful gloomily. "She said she wants to lend Father her witch-cook, for she has one who is very good with strengthening broths. But you know what a gossip she is."

"Send her away," said Stephen. "Say the Admiral can't receive. Family only."

"She is family, at least she's some sort of connection," replied Truthful. "Not quite a distant enough one."

"Then it will be all over the county in a week, and the metropolis the week after," said Edmund. "Think of what it will do to Mama!"

Everyone fell silent at that, for Lady Newington-Lacy was a dear parent to her sons, and in many ways a surrogate mother for Truthful.

"Very good punch," said Robert.

"Oh, do be quiet, Robert!" begged Truthful.

"There's only one thing to do," said Edmund, drawing himself up to his full height, only spoiling the effect a little by staggering against the wall. "Emerald's been stolen by a damned storm-sprite or something, beg pardon, Truthful, naughty, I mean naughty storm-sprite. Never get it back from one of them. So I must go forth and find an acceptable substitute. Family honor and all that."

"Oh, I am sure no one will *really* think you stole it. . . ." Truthful began, but an image of Lady Troutbridge flashed across her mind, and she realized others would think the worst. Lady Troutbridge would be delighted to believe the scandal, and would repeat it.

"No other way, Newt," said Edmund, making a

grandiloquent and rash gesture that nearly undid his precarious regained balance. "No other way. I shall leave tomorrow! Yes, tomorrow. Or the day after. And I will not return unless it is with a gem of equal beauty and monetary worth."

"Flummery," said Stephen. "I will *divine* the location of *your* Emerald! Have to consult old Flammarion in Paris, I expect. Expert on cloud-catchers and that ilk. Or the Greek fellow in Constantinople. Magister Makanios. Start tomorrow. Or the day after."

"You want a new emerald?" asked Robert dreamily. "Mine one! Why, there's a flooded shaft in Golconda just needs pumping out, and a steam donkey is just the way to do it. I'll go there, fix it up, fetch you a new Emerald!"

"Where is Golconda?" asked Truthful uneasily.

"India," said Robert. "Wonder if they have punch there?"

"That's settled then," said Edmund. He sat back down, looked alarmed as the chair proved lower than expected, and grabbed at the air. Coughing to cover his embarrassment, he added, "I'll go to China. Bound to be emeralds lying about the place there. You'll get an emerald one way or another, Newt!"

"Oh no!" exclaimed Truthful. "You can't all go away! Think of your mother!"

"Glad to see us away from the scandal," said Edmund breezily.

"Only be away a year," added Stephen. "Nothing to it."

"Back in an ant's whisker," said Robert. "And I shan't have to return to Harrow."

"If you are going to search for the Emerald or a replacement," said Truthful, "then so must I."

"Ridiculous!" snapped Edmund.

"Unnecessary, my dear Newt," said Stephen.

"Waste of good punch . . . I mean time," announced Robert.

All three glared at her, their rum-affected countenances rather more florid than would normally be the case. Truthful bowed her head under their very brotherly approbation. Truly, she felt like their pet name for her: a newt, under the gaze of several large, sanctimonious, and more senior amphibians.

"It just seems to me," she said in a small voice, "I could go looking for the Emerald in London. Someone could have sent that cloud-catcher to steal it, you know, and then they'd have to try and sell it somewhere. I thought I could go early to Great-aunt Ermintrude, I was going next month anyway, for my coming-out. . . ."

"Oh, London," said Edmund, in a relieved tone. "That's different."

"No harm in Newt going to London," added Stephen. "Most sensible. Might even discover something."

"Lot of steam donkeys in London," muttered Robert. "Experimental Railway. The Hordern Press. That exacavatin' circulator thing . . ."

"All the places you mentioned are very far away," said Truthful doubtfully. "Are you sure you should be going?"

All three young men laughed, caught up in the dream of adventure.

"Must do something," declared Edmund.

"Hear him, hear him," joined in the brothers.

"Should have a toast," said Robert, struggling to his feet.

Truthful interposed herself between him and the punch bowl.

"A toast with coffee!" she said. "It will be here directly!"

"Can't toast with coffee," grumbled Robert, but he shambled back and fell into his chair.

Truthful looked anxiously at the door and wondered why the coffee was taking so long. She had to distract her cousins somehow. If only she'd thought to ask Jukes to take the punch bowl away!

"I shall miss you very much, you know," said Truthful. "You are so much more to me than mere cousins. I shall always think of you as brothers!"

"Of course," said Stephen, as if Truthful had just stated the most commonplace fact.

"Might as well *be* our sister," exclaimed Edmund. "Still see you in my . . . what's it called, memory thing . . . like a window . . ."

"Mind's eye?" suggested Truthful.

"That's the article! See you in my mind's eye in a pair of Stephen's old breeches, your pigtail done up Navy-fashion by Hetherington, with your front tooth missing, both front teeth, and the freckles, oh lore, remember the freckles—"

"Don't look like that now though," interrupted Stephen. Even in his current rum-addled state he perceived that some of this fraternal honesty was damaging Truthful's pride. "But having thought of you as a sister since we were in short pants . . . might as well be a sister. I mean our sister."

"Going to marry a marquis at least," said Stephen.

"Who?" asked Truthful.

"You," said Stephen. "Top of the tree for Newt."

"Don't be ridiculous," replied Truthful, laughing. "I have no desire to marry a marquis. Or anyone! Particularly not now."

"Thought you were looking forward to being presented and all that," said Edmund. "Surprised. Bored by it all myself. Almack's very dull. Balls very dull. Frightful crushes. Some of those girls were positively terrifying. And their mothers! Take Lady Godalming for example—"

"I *was* looking forward to coming out," said Truthful,

interrupting the flow of what looked to be a compromising anecdote. "But it is of no consequence now. Finding the Emerald is all that matters."

"Or a reasonable substitute," said Edmund. He fumbled at the fob pocket of his waistcoat and produced his watch. "Good God, it's late! We must be off at once."

"No, no," exclaimed Truthful. "You must have some coffee first. And surely none of you will go without saying farewell to your mother!"

"Farewell?" asked Edmund. "Going to see her now! Gave us strict instructions to be back by two!"

"Won't leave on our . . . our *quest* till tomorrow," said Stephen. "Or the day after."

"We'll have to tell Father," said Edmund thoughtfully. "He won't be happy, but . . ."

"There's simply nothing else to be done," growled Stephen, in a fair imitation of his father's voice, uttering one of that worthy's frequent maxims.

They all laughed at this, Truthful's silvery peals sounding over the top of the deeper laughter of the young men. She was to remember that moment of laughter all her life, and the way it echoed out into the clear Spring morning, for it heralded the beginning of her own adventures.

THE SEARCH BEGINS

Truthful left for London the next day, accompanied by Agatha, an ancient groom called Tom, and an only slightly younger footman called Smith. The Admiral still lay out of his senses most of the time, but he swam into consciousness every now and again, long enough to understand that Truthful was going early to his aunt Ermintrude, and he approved.

Agatha had not approved, of course, but she came around after several hours of coaxing from Truthful. "Lunnon" was not a good place, she said, but a breeding ground for wickedness and a veritable stage for the display of all kinds of vice and depravity. Truthful countered this with the fact that they would be part of the household of Lady Ermintrude Badgery, who was, she felt sure, an absolute model of propriety. Agatha gave a strange half smile, half scowl when Truthful said this, but uttered no further protest.

It did not occur to Truthful that she could have merely ordered Agatha to accompany her to London or leave her service. The maid had been with her since she was ten, and had to some degree achieved a kind of grumpy superiority over her mistress.

But Truthful's coaxing did the trick. Agatha was at her side as the young lady looked out the window of her father's rather ancient and distinctly unmodish post chaise and four, holding the strap as the conveyance rattled and lurched its way along the London road.

At first, the novelty of traveling without her father sustained Truthful, but that was soon replaced by a weariness brought on by the discomfort and the total lack of conversation from Agatha, who sat silently next to her, doubtless brooding on the evil city that lay ahead.

After several hours of travel, Truthful's weariness gave way to a troubled sleep filled with dreams of the Emerald, which became a great glowing green fire and then turned into the Admiral's staring, fevered face, his mouth working and virulent accusations growing louder and louder. His voice seemed to fill Truthful's head with angry shouts until she suddenly woke and realized there *was* shouting, but they were shouts of alarm, not of anger.

For a muzzy second Truthful wondered where she was. Even as she realized she was in the carriage, the vehicle tilted over at an alarming angle and there was a resounding crack from something breaking behind them. Truthful was flung to the floor, Agatha fell against her, and then they were both hurled against the door as the coach came to an abrupt halt and rolled over onto its side, accompanied by the panicked neighing of the horses and the shouts of the footman and groom.

Truthful lay stunned for a moment, then pulled herself out from underneath a semiconscious Agatha and climbed up the now vertical bench, using the leather hand straps to good advantage. She struggled with the door for a moment, flung it open like a hatch, and popped her head out, only to have her hair blow back in her face in a most disorderly way, her bonnet having slid to the back of her head. Below her, Agatha raised herself up on one elbow and hissed, "Lunnon!"

But Truthful saw they were still in the country and many miles from London. Their coach had been run off the road and into a ditch adjoining a large pasture, and was the subject of much attention from half a dozen curious cows. A little farther on, a mail coach was also turned over in the ditch on the other side of the road, and people were climbing out of it (or picking themselves off the road, having fallen from the roof). There were a lot of fists being shaken and numerous epithets directed at an old gentleman in a disreputable driving coat. The coachman, Truthful thought, and clearly the man responsible for the accident.

At that moment, Smith the footman saw Truthful perched precariously half out of the carriage door and hurried over.

"Are you all right, milady?" he asked anxiously.

"Yes, thank you, Smith," replied Truthful calmly. "But what has happened to Tom?"

"I'm here, milady," said a voice from the front of the coach, followed by the emergence of the angry groom. "If we don't have two of the horses lame at least, if not worse, it'll be a surprise, and thank heaven they're not the Admiral's own! There just wasn't anything I could do, milady. I do beg your pardon."

"Don't worry, Tom," said Truthful. "I can see what must have happened. The road is far too narrow here, and on a bend, too! I thought the mail coaches were driven more carefully than the common stage, but I see that is not the case!"

"Well, for the most part they are, milady," said Smith.

"But I reckon it weren't one of the regular coachmen at the reins. That old gadger there probably paid them off in gin to let him ply the whip. I saw him at the last change a-buying them blue ruin or somesuch."

"Paid them off in gin!" exclaimed Truthful, much shocked. "I am sure that is distinctly against the law, and clearly very dangerous to all concerned. I shall have a word to say to that fellow."

She started to climb farther out the door, but got stuck till Smith climbed up and lifted her out and handed her down to Tom, much as they had done when she was a small child, for both were old family retainers, albeit representing two generations in the Newington service.

She had just got firmly on the ground and was in the process of dealing with her bonnet and recalcitrant hair when the old "coachman" hurried over, crying out, "How-de-do! I do beg your pardon, ma'am. A most unfortunate miscalculation. No one hurt, I trust?"

"That no one has been hurt is due more to good fortune than anything else," said Truthful sternly. "I intend to report you to the relevant authorities at the next town. Bribing mail coachmen to let you drive and crashing a mail coach into another conveyance is surely a most serious crime."

"Oh, the authorities know all about me," said the old man cheerfully. "Besides, I *am* the authorities in these parts. You could report me to me, I suppose. No? I would prefer it if you allow me to assist you on your way, and make some slight amends for the trouble I've caused. Who do I have the honor to address?"

"I am Lady Truthful Newington," said Truthful, rather taken aback by the man's cheerfulness and obvious good breeding, even though he wore strange clothes and had a trace of some peculiar accent. "My father is Admiral the Viscount Newington. And you, sir?"

"Charmed," replied the old man. "I'm Otterbrook, don't you know."

"Oh," said Truthful. "It is an honor to meet you, my Lord Marquis."

She had read about Lord Otterbrook, the fourth Marquis of Poole. He was known as the "colonial peer." A rank outsider for the title, he had been a remittance man in the Americas, the Orient, and finally the colony of New South Wales, succeeding to the title only when the main line of the family managed to get themselves all killed in various land and Naval battles and hunting accidents. It was said the last marquis had died of apoplexy at the thought that his eccentric cousin would inherit after all. Particularly as his successor was merely an indifferent diviner, rather than possessing any of the more socially acceptable magics of glamour or persuasion.

"What seems to be the damage, hmmm?" inquired the Marquis, pacing around the carriage to look at the underside. "Ah, a broken axle. And your leaders lamed? I shall have to convey you myself, Lady Truthful. My curricle should be along shortly."

Truthful felt a blush rising across her neck at his words. Here was someone old enough to be her grandfather trying to compromise her reputation before she even arrived in London!

"Oh no, that won't do, will it," added Lord Otterbrook suddenly, seeing her color. "Forgot. Respectability and all that. Couldn't fit your maid anyway. By the bye, where is your maid? Or respectable aunt, or whatever. Must have one tucked away somewhere, what?"

"Oh dear!" exclaimed Truthful. "My maid. She's still inside. Agatha! Are you all right?"

There was a deathly silence for a moment, then Agatha's voice came grumbling out the open door.

"I might be better if we weren't a-going to Lunnon—and perhaps we ain't."

"Quick, Tom, Smith—help Agatha out. Oh, I am sorry, Agatha!"

She turned around just in time to see the glint of yellow metal and the two men pocketing something. They ducked their heads guiltily at her and climbed back into the carriage to assist Agatha.

"Just a little ointment for their hurts, physical and spiritual," said Lord Otterbrook, chuckling. "Gold works wonders for anything short of broken bones. Even broken bones, sometimes. I have decided that I shall send a post chaise back from Maidstone for you, though it may take some little while."

"You are most kind, sir," replied Truthful, somewhat stiffly. She still felt it was all his fault that she had been delayed at all.

"I know, my dear," commiserated Lord Otterbrook. "You think I'm a silly old fool who's quite queered your entire journey. Well, I shall have to make my amends. What can I—"

The sound of horses on the road and the blast of a horn behind him interrupted the old man, and he turned to look over his shoulder. A curricle rounded the bend with a pair of high-stepping thoroughbreds perfectly under the one-handed control of the tiger, a boy groom in striped livery who was about to blow another peal on his horn. The peal sounded, he dropped the trumpet to hang from its lanyard, and brought the vehicle to a beautiful two-handed halt between the overturned carriages.

"A proper mess you've made of it, milord," said the tiger, critically surveying the wreckage. Though he couldn't have been more than thirteen, his face showed all the scorn of a true whip for the cack-handed. "I did warn you. Top-heavy, I said, and not at all the article you're used to. And you supposed to be able to see tomorrow before it happens and all—"

"Yes. Yes. You were quite right, Gully," interrupted Otterbrook genially. "Now, we must get on to Maidstone and arrange a carriage for this young lady. Lady Truthful, I most humbly beg your pardon. I shall send a coach as soon as I may."

He heaved himself up beside his tiger and added, "Please present my compliments to your father and recall me to him. Say I remember the house fire very well."

"You know my father?" asked Truthful, surprised. The Admiral was not a sociable person. "And a house fire, I think you said?"

"Yes," replied the Marquis. "We met in America. We watched their White House burn together. Rather an imposing sight. He said he would rather it was *Carlton* House burning. Ha! Ha!"

Truthful blushed at this reference to the Prince Regent's London home.

"I'm afraid my father and the Duke of Clarence have a feud going back to when my father was a lieutenant in the West Indies and the Duke a midshipman. Unfortunately

Father also holds the Duke's brothers in low esteem, including the Prince Regent."

"Well, no harm in that," said the eccentric peer. "I hold him in low esteem myself, for all he's a friend of mine! He means well, but he ain't got much up top. Good-bye!"

The curricle sprang away, rapidly accelerating past those passengers of the mail coach who had decided to walk on instead of waiting for the next passing vehicle or a replacement coach to come from Maidstone.

A snort behind her recalled Truthful to the emergence of Agatha, who had just descended with the aid of the two hard-pressed male servants.

"Hardly out of the 'ouse and this happens," grumbled Agatha. "It'll get worse, milady. Mark my words."

Indeed, thought Truthful, it did get worse. Agatha grumbled without pause for the two hours they waited for the post chaise. She grumbled for the half hour it took to transfer their luggage, and she only stopped grumbling when the carriage moved off because the motion, so she said, made her feel so ill she couldn't speak.

It was a very tiring journey, and near midnight before they came to London. Truthful was almost too tired to marvel at the lights of the Gas Light and Coke Company, or at the crowds who were still abroad when all good country folk would be well abed.

But at last they came to Lady Ermintrude Badgery's imposing house in Grosvenor Square, and were met by Dworkin, the anxious butler, and a flurry of footmen and maids, and Truthful at least was immediately transferred to a large, ostentatious room wallpapered in green and silver and completely dominated by the most comfortable of feather beds.

LADY BADGERY'S FEZ

The next day dawned bright and cheery, but Truthful was not awake to see it. By the time she came down to an elevenish breakfast, clouds had rolled across and a slight drizzle had begun. Truthful ate a rather lackluster poached egg, looked at the rain outside, and felt gloomy. London was not living up to its promised allure. To make matters worse, Agatha had decided to have one of her turns and had taken to her bed, and the replacement maid had none of her skill with hair or dress. Consequently Truthful was wearing a not particularly well-ironed walking dress of sprig muslin and a half bonnet to hide her hair, and felt a complete dowd.

Soon after she finished her breakfast, a footman brought her a note on aquamarine paper folded into the shape of a cocked hat. It was, Truthful soon discovered, a request from her great-aunt, asking her to call upon her in her bedchamber, as she was feeling indisposed and would not be coming down.

Truthful climbed the stairs with some trepidation. She had known her great-aunt Ermintrude reasonably well as a child, but had not seen her aged relative for many years, due to her frequent indispositions and consequent aversion to travel. That aversion might have spread from travel to include great-nieces, thought Truthful as she knocked, and then opened, the door to Lady Badgery's bedchamber.

She had expected a dark sickroom lined with bottles of medicine and obscure medical instruments, perhaps even a jar of leeches. But the room was bright with the new gaslights, which illuminated strange Oriental wall hangings and a huge bed hung with gauzy curtains. Even the window was a departure from traditional practice, for it was open and Truthful could feel cool moist air coming through it.

Then the gauzy curtains twitched aside, revealing a little old lady propped up on a pile of gold-embroidered cushions of red plush. She wore a simple nightshirt, but her head was adorned with a very large red fez, complete with a long golden tassel. A pile of letters lay on the coverlet in front of her next to a wicked-looking curved Turkish knife that she was employing as a letter opener.

Lady Badgery looked up as Truthful closed the door behind her, and her blue-black eyes ran up and down her in appraisal. Apparently satisfied by what she saw, she put her current letter down and said, "Truthful, my dear niece. Parkins! Don't be such a jobberknoll, and fetch Lady Truthful a chair."

At first Truthful wasn't sure who Lady Badgery was talking to, then a blue bow appeared from the floor on the other side of the bed, followed by the head of the large elderly woman whose head it adorned. This was Parkins, her great-aunt's maid and constant companion. She straightened up to her full height and placed a knife scabbard on the side table.

"Milady will throw the scabbard about," she said affectionately as she trod heavily around the foot of the bed and moved a chair three inches closer to Lady Badgery.

"There we are, Lady Truthful. And may I say it's a pleasure to see you all grown up, and beautiful, too."

"No you may not!" exclaimed Lady Badgery. "Go and fetch us some tea."

"Yes, milady," replied Parkins, executing a rather sarcastic curtsy and winking at Truthful as she left.

"Been with me since I was married," said Lady Badgery.

"Never could do a thing with her. Sit down, girl, do!"

Truthful sat down and tried not to stare at her great-aunt's fez. Now that she looked closely, she could also see that Lady Badgery was wearing at least a dozen rune-inscribed spell-breaking silver bracelets on each arm—and that certainly couldn't be the sort of thing a model of propriety would display!

"Don't worry, my dear," said Lady Badgery, catching her gaze. "The fez is a gift from an old friend; it has certain powers to help concentrate the mind. I don't wear it in company. Callers and the outside world find me to be very proper indeed."

"Oh, I see," said Truthful. "Like playacting at home with friends."

"Something of the sort," replied Lady Badgery easily. "But what brings you here so urgently, child? I wasn't expecting you for weeks, the Season has barely begun. And without your father . . . you hinted at some dark news in your letter. I must confess I have been unable to scry what has occurred and so await with burning ears!"

"It *is* terrible news, Great-aunt," burst out Truthful. "The Newington Emerald has been lost! Or . . . or stolen!"

"Really?" asked Lady Badgery, lifting one aristocratic eyebrow beneath her fez. "What a curious thing. Now, dear, don't be upset. It is, after all, only a sort of rock with some sorcery attached."

"Papa says it is the luck of the Newingtons," said Truthful sorrowfully. "And it is a very powerful talisman, much more powerful than is generally supposed."

"He must really be ill," replied Lady Badgery. "He never cared for it much before, and your mother didn't like it at all. As for the stone's vaunted powers, she certainly never displayed them. She said it was too heavy to wear, and it felt like the proverbial millstone."

"Really?" asked Truthful. She smiled at the thought of wearing an actual millstone. She had rarely heard stories about her mother, and remembered little herself.

"The absolute truth," replied Lady Badgery. "She married into the family, and thought emeralds did not particularly suit her color, though she was wrong in that respect. Nor was she much interested in magic, save for her own particular gifts. Now tell me exactly how the Emerald has been lost . . . or stolen."

Truthful leaned forward a little in her chair, and her great-aunt leaned toward her from the bed so that the tassel on the red fez of the old lady almost touched Truthful's bonnet. In this conspiratorial posture, Truthful told Lady Badgery the tale of the storm, the showing of the Emerald, its subsequent loss, and the Admiral's sickness and suspicions. When she had finished, Lady Badgery lay back in her bed and chuckled.

"A merry pickle," she said. "And not easily untangled, I'll warrant. What do you hope to do, my dear?"

"Well," faltered Truthful, "I was hoping you might advise me, Great-aunt . . . I know you are a sorceress. I thought you might be able to scry for the Emerald—"

"Can't scry for a magical talisman, particularly if it *is* a powerful one," snorted Lady Badgery. "You should know that. What did your father pay that tutor for?"

"Oh, I'd forgotten," said Truthful. "You know I was never much for academic magic, Great-aunt."

"Nor was I, as a girl," said Lady Badgery. "What book learning I have came later. One thing I did learn early on was not to put all my trust in magic. If it *can* be done without magic, it's *better* done without magic."

"Perhaps I might call upon jewellers and pawnbrokers and so forth to see if any large, sorcerous stones have been offered for sale—"

"That's impossible in this censorious age," sighed Lady Badgery. "You haven't even come out yet! Wandering around London, talking to pawnbrokers! You would be sunk before launching. Why, you're barely out of the schoolroom, Miss!"

"I might disguise myself," suggested Truthful half-heartedly. "I have to do something!"

"Disguise . . ." mused Lady Badgery, her old eyes suddenly alight with scheming pleasure. "Perhaps your notion isn't as wild as I first thought, Truthful."

She tapped the top of her fez and began to sort through the letters in front of her, selecting one that was cut open, evidently already read that morning. The old lady flicked it open, ran her eyes across it, and then pounced with a thin finger on a particular line.

"*Cousin Henri est entré au monastère voisin, comme nous nous y sommes toujours préparés. Une triste vie pour un de Vienne, vous en conviendrez, mon cousin. Mais c'est un fils cadet, un homme pieux et doux, et il a le teint si frais qu' on pourrait le prendre pour une femme. En outre, il a toujours été solitare . . .*"[1] she read with relish. "I trust you speak good French, Truthful?"

"*Oui, madame. J'en ai fait une étude particulière,*"[2] replied Truthful, who had always enjoyed her French lessons with a succession of tutors, including an émigré noblewoman who had told many tales of pre-Revolution Versailles and Paris to her eager student and even some torrid tales of Napoleon Bonaparte's rise to power and his unique ability to bespell both individuals and huge crowds so that it was only safe

---

1 "Cousin Henri has entered the monastery nearby, as we always expected. A sad life for a de Vienne, I think you will agree, cousin. But he is a younger son, a pious and gentle man, and so fresh-faced he could be mistaken for a woman. Further, he has always been reclusive."

2 "Yes, madame. I have made a particular study."

to look at him via a mirror. "But I don't understand. Who is Henri de Vienne?"

"The nephew of a cousin of mine," said Lady Badgery. "As you heard, a shy and womanly young man, of pious disposition and retiring habit . . . who has just become a monk. He will do very well."

"For what, Great-aunt?"

"For you to impersonate," exclaimed Lady Badgery triumphantly. "Lady Truthful Newington cannot search London for an emerald, but her French relation Henri de Vienne can certainly do so on her behalf!"

"But I don't think . . ." said Truthful. "I'm not sure. . . . Do you think I can be disguised as a man?"

"Bah! The disguise itself is nothing," replied Lady Badgery. "A little sorcery, a bandeau pulled tight . . . It is the behavior that is most difficult . . . that is, according to accounts . . . or so I believe. You were brought up with the Newington-Lacy boys—played with them, talked to them—just pretend you are one of them. Any difficulties you may have can be explained away because you are French and destined to be a religious. Oh, this will be capital fun!"

"But I've never been to France!" protested Truthful. "And I have no skill with glamour myself, and I will need clothes—"

"Bah again!" cried Lady Badgery. "Henri probably only

ever knew his family's chateau and a few towns, which I shall describe to you. You shall say you never went to Paris due to your religious feelings and a natural antipathy to Bonaparte's regime! As for clothes, we shall take your measurements and order suitable garb, my dear. It is fortunate you are slim. And with regard to glamour, while my own poor bones are now too old to take a spell, I have not lost my expertise, nor thrown away my apparatus."

"Oh," said Truthful, blushing. She had forgotten that her great-aunt was a famous glamouress, among her other magical accomplishments. "If you really think I can . . . and if it will help find the Emerald . . . I'll do it."

"Excellent!" Lady Badgery beamed. "Now, where is the tea?"

An hour later, to Truthful's bewilderment, everything was settled for her to assume the identity of Henri de Vienne. For some of the time, at least. Lady Badgery had decided that despite Truthful's late arrival the night before, many people would have heard she was in London, for as she said, servants talk. So Lady Truthful must be in residence, happily at the same time as her French cousin, ostensibly as a last-ditch effort on the part of his father to expose him to the world before he committed himself to the Church. If word leaked out that the young Henri de Vienne was searching for the Newington Emerald, everyone would presume he was helping his unfortunate cousin, the Admiral being unwell.

Her measurements being taken by Parkins, who showed surprising familiarity with male attire, orders had sped to Weston in Conduit Street for coats, Hoby (at the top of St. James) for boots, and the finest linen to match. In all cases, the countess attached a note giving detailed measurements and drawn outlines of Truthful's feet and hands accompanied by the annotation that they were for her soon-to-arrive cousin, the overtly religious Chevalier de Vienne, who preferred not to be called upon for fitting due to a reluctance to wear "finery." The clothes were to be a present to the young man from the countess, who hoped to remove him from his sombre clerical garb, even suggesting that the young man had an unfortunate preference for that most awful of garments, the cassock.

That story, said Lady Badgery, would be all over London within a week, and would explain both the lack of personal attendance from tailors, bootmakers, and the like, and perhaps many other oddities as well.

"In the meantime, my dear," said Lady Badgery, "we must decide what is to be done with Lady Truthful. I had planned on giving a ball here for you, but perhaps that should be left for a little while. . . . It would be difficult to explain even a monklike cousin's absence from my own ball if he is supposed to be staying here. However, I am sure there will be no shortage of invitations for you in any case. We must present you at Almack's, of course. Fortunately, Lady Jersey will certainly provide you with vouchers. Doubtless she would do so for my sake alone, but she was also very fond of your father's older brother."

"Oh, yes! Almack's!" said Truthful. "That is of the first importance, is it not? I recall a verse to that effect."

"Yes," agreed Lady Badgery. "Luttrell's, no doubt: 'If once to Almack's you belong / Like monarchs you can do no wrong / But banished thence on Wednesday night / By Jove, you can do nothing right.' He is an amusing man—you shall probably meet him, he often dines with Lady Holland, who is a dear friend of mine."

<hr />

For the next three days, Truthful and Lady Badgery remained quietly at home in Grosvenor Square, despite Truthful's natural desire to see at least the Tower and some of the sights, and attend a play, particularly as Edmund Keane was performing at Drury Lane. But her great-aunt insisted that she must perfect her role as Henri de Vienne, and kept her busy memorizing the details of the Château de Vienne and the land about it, practicing her French, and getting used to masculine attire, which was now arriving at a steady pace in attractive brown paper parcels.

Lady Badgery also insisted that Truthful keep her

intended deception secret, even from Agatha. As Agatha was still keeping to her bed (claiming "Lunnon" had brought on a semipermanent sick headache) this wasn't hard. Parkins and Lady Badgery herself assisted Truthful to dress, displaying a knowledge of male clothing that Truthful found rather shocking.

Though Truthful was slim, a bandeau was found to not be sufficiently secure in flattening her chest. So she had to wear a corset under her shirt, a lighter version similar to the one made popular by the Prince Regent. Fortunately, as it was not holding back a similar bulk it didn't creak with every movement, and as Lady Badgery said, if it did become noticeable, it could always be explained away as a religious observance, akin to a hair shirt.

Her hair presented another problem, but they managed to arrive at a compromise cut long enough to still be dressed in many of the current female modes, but not long enough to be considered strange in a man—particularly a Frenchman, for whom there would be made a condescending allowance.

The final piece of disguise was provided by Lady Badgery, who set a powerful glamour upon Truthful so onlookers would see her as a man. Because the spell would have to be taken on and off frequently, it was decided to place it upon a very real-looking artificial moustache, which Truthful fixed to her upper lip with gum arabic. In her full rig-out and with the ensorcelled moustache in place, Parkins and Lady Badgery assured her she looked very much the young gentleman, even under the full glare of the sun. But her great-aunt warned her that without the moustache and the glamour it held, her costume alone would probably only serve in dim light, or at a distance.

All callers were turned away in this time with the news that Lady Badgery was indisposed and her great-niece still wearied by the journey and an unfortunate coach mishap. Lord Otterbrook's role in the accident was not mentioned.

Truthful, studying the cards the callers left and listening to Dworkin recite their verbal messages, was pleasantly surprised to find a large number of highly eligible young men asking after her health and general well-being. But she was soon disabused of any notion of their gallantry or her own allure by Lady Badgery, who looked over their names and sniffed.

"Fortune hunters. They know you're worth at least ten thousand a year from your mother, even without your father's estates. Not to mention heiress to the Newington Emerald, which they must not know is missing . . . which is curious, now that I think on it."

"It is very odd," said Truthful, her brow troubled. "Lady Troutbridge *did* call upon Father that afternoon, and he was awake, if still wandering in his wits. I am sure he would have spoken of its disappearance *and* blamed the Newington-Lacys. I wonder why she hasn't spread the tale."

"The only reason she would not is if she is ill or the story would somehow reflect badly on herself," replied Lady Badgery. "Otherwise, Portia Troutbridge has never been known to keep a scandal to herself."

"Oh, I do hope she is ill!" exclaimed Truthful. "I mean, only just ill enough to keep the news quiet for a little longer. Is that too dreadful of me?"

"Not at all," announced Lady Badgery. "It is a very reasonable desire. In the case of Portia Troutbridge I myself would wish for something much more severe. Scarlet fever, perhaps. Or the plague."

At last, on the evening of the fifth day after Truthful's arrival, it was time to put their plan into action. Truthful, her moustache glued on, donned a low-crowned beaver and traveling clothes of a very plain cut, covered them with an old and very unfashionable single-caped driving coat that had belonged to the late Lord Badgery, crept out of the servant's entrance at midnight, and walked around the corner to Charles Street, taking care that no one observed her. There, she waited a few minutes till the hackney cab the countess's intermediaries had ordered approached. Its driver, seeing a single gentleman standing on the corner, drew up and leaned down.

"You the gent who's to go across to Park Lane and then back to the Square?" he asked hoarsely.

"Yes," she muttered, keeping her voice low, and hat well down, shading her face.

"Right. Well, jump up, sir."

Truthful, who had been waiting to be handed up, started, then jumped in as best she could. There was straw on the floor of the cab and she brushed her boots down automatically, thinking of how awful it would be to arrive anywhere with the telltale straw of a hackney on one's costume.

The drive to Park Lane and then along it was a nervous one for Truthful, who had never thought to be alone in a cab at midnight, in the middle of London . . . and dressed as a man!

But the drive was uneventful. They passed several other carriages, a group of lantern-bearing street-keepers gathered at the Grosvenor Gate into Hyde Park, and a number of tipsy young gentlemen who were trying to walk backward along the full length of Park Lane, apparently for a bet, as they were urged on by a number of others who were walking the normal way beside them.

Ten minutes later the hackney pulled up outside Lady Badgery's house and Truthful jumped down. She turned back for a moment to hand the driver a guinea, a massive overpayment were it not for the added gruff instruction: "Forget you came here this evening."

Then she was knocking on the door—a firm but polite knock, which she felt might reflect the character of a religious-minded young gentleman.

After five minutes had produced no discernible effect on the other side of the door, she knocked again. The door opened, presenting the cautious visage of the elder footman, with the second footman behind him holding a stout cudgel. Before they could speak, Truthful gruffly proclaimed her new identity.

"I am the Chevalier Henri de Vienne, cousin to Lady Badgery. I believe I am expected."

5

MAJOR HARNETT'S MANUSCRIPT

The next few days passed in a rush of activity for both of Truthful's personas. As Lady Truthful Newington, she drove out to Hyde Park with Lady Badgery in her barouche at the fashionable hour between five and six, thereupon meeting many of the dowager's friends and not a few young gallants; she visited the dowager's modiste and ordered several gowns of the latest fashion; made two morning visits to family friends; attended one very modest, well-bred, and yawn-inducing evening card party; and received a great number of callers.

The Chevalier de Vienne ostensibly spent most of his

time secluded in one of the upper bedchambers in silent contemplation and prayer. But when Lady Truthful was resting between excursions or guests, the Chevalier rode out to call upon the jewelers of London. The servants, noticing the care he took to avoid "meeting" Truthful, thought him very shy. The grooms, noting his unsteady seat when riding astride, put it down to his being French. Truthful was a fine horsewoman, but she was used to a sidesaddle.

Armed with explanatory letters from Lady Truthful and Lady Badgery, the elegant young Frenchman was met with unvarying politeness and differing degrees of unctuousness by the jewelers, but none proved of any help. The matter was not made easier because Truthful could not come straight out and talk about the Newington Emerald, but only inquire about any particularly large and sorcerous stones they might have heard were suddenly for sale. But apart from the relatively regular reappearance of the cursed Calendula Diamond, no large and sorcerous jewels had surfaced among the more reputable jewelers, and the less respectable (who hinted at underworld connections) were no more use. Nearly all the jewelers tried to sell the young Frenchman something from their own stock, and indeed she was tempted by a number of items that were not only beautiful, but imbued with minor charms.

Truthful was riding back from just such a meeting when

she took a wrong turning, and then another. Fortunately a watchman came up behind her and, seeing a young, foreign-looking gentleman gazing about in consternation, directed her attention to the dome of St. Paul's as a useful landmark and told her to take the next road on the left.

But this turning brought her to a lane that was crowded with the business of paper and books. Men were carrying quires of paper, loading them onto carts; others were transporting paper-wrapped packages of what could only be books. Here and there, men of a more scholarly look moved through doorways or down sunken steps.

It was very much a scene of industry, and Truthful felt certain that her immaculate coat of blue superfine, buckskin pantaloons, and black Hessian top boots would not survive passage unmarked. Nervously, she began to wheel her horse around, still gazing back at the workmen, some of whom returned her gaze in what she thought was a threatening manner.

She had almost brought the horse about when it suddenly shied, and she looked back to her front in horror as a man leaped away from under the horse's forefeet, dropping paper everywhere and cursing.

"Damn it, man!" he cried, staring up at Truthful as she leaned forward to calm her mount, muttering soothing words in French. As always, the horse responded more to her innate sorcery than any words, and quietened immediately.

"Sir!" exclaimed the man again, his voice loud with anger. "I ask you to look at me when I am speaking to you!"

Truthful leaned back in the saddle, her mount now calm and steady. Shutting her eyes for an instant, she thought of what her cousins would do in a similar circumstance. Then she opened her eyes and looked down.

The man was staring furiously up at her, brandishing a wad of papers in his hand and gesturing at others lying ruined on the street—churned into the muddy cobbles, or cut by the horse's hooves. He was coatless, and Truthful saw that his shirt was both crumpled and ink-stained, and his breeches and boots deserved better care. He looked to be some six or seven years older than herself, and his features, if not set in anger, could be described as handsome. He had a particularly fine shock of jet-black hair.

Truthful saw him like a picture for a moment, then the sound and anger washed back over her, and she thought of her cousin's tales of similar encounters.

"I am looking at you, sir," she said, in her deepest and most French-sounding voice. "And I am sorry I have ruined your papers. Would a guinea cover the damage?"

She reached in her waistcoat pocket for the coin, but this mollifying action only seemed to enrage the man still further.

"It would be a sorry day if I let a Frenchman trammel my *Badajoz Diary* into the road," he said coldly. "Dismount, sir, and I'll teach you a lesson in manners, if not horsemanship!"

Truthful stared down at his set face and fought back an urge to cry. No one had ever spoken to her like that before, but fear soon gave way to her own anger.

"It is not in my nature to partake in fisticuffs with any . . . paper carrier or clerk," she said equally coldly. "I am the Chevalier de Vienne, not some common—"

"This is England," interrupted the man, stepping closer and seizing her stirrup. "And here you'll find a duke wouldn't turn aside from a proper turn-up with a potboy, let alone a paper carrier, if the occasion warranted it. So if you won't step down, Monsoor Chevalier, I'll turn you from your horse for my lesson!"

"As you wish," replied Truthful, ire and trepidation mingling together in her butterflying stomach. Whoever the man was, he spoke very well, and was obviously no paper carrier. She dismounted, the horse between them, and looked back over the saddle. He was almost a head taller than Truthful, and only her high-crowned hat took her to near his size.

"I hope you remember that it was not I who chose this quarrel, but an accident," she began, stepping out from behind her mount and raising her fists in the manner the Newington-Lacys had tried to teach her on several occasions, and that she had seen on her disguised excursions with them to various mills and less formal demonstrations of fisticuffs.

"Indeed," said the man. He stepped forward likewise, and raised two large and very solid-looking fists. Truthful trembled as he did so, but she didn't retreat, and looked him squarely in the eye.

"Please don't mark my face," she said suddenly, thinking of the difficulties a black eye would raise for Lady Truthful. She clenched her fists again at the thought, presenting a slim boyish figure with a fighting stance as open as a door.

"I don't think I can hit you at all," replied the man, lowering his hands. "You're a plucky devil, lad, but you're not up to my weight. It'd be like striking a child."

"I'm thankful for that, sir," said Truthful honestly, dropping her own guard. "I *am* sorry I made you drop those papers. They are not too important, I trust?"

"That all depends on whom you might ask!" laughed the man, all traces of rage melting from his face. "It is my account of the Siege of Badajoz. The final manuscript. I was just taking it to my publishers, when I am beset by a Frenchman! Now I shall have to copy or rewrite at least two score of the pages!"

"Again, I beg your pardon," said Truthful, bending down to help him pick up the fallen pages. As she passed them to him, one caught her eye. The title page, torn in half, but with *Badajoz Diary—by a Soldier* penned in an elegant script, and under that "Major Harnett, 95th Rifles."

"You are Major Harnett?" she blurted out, as he took the page, frowning at its condition.

"I was a soldier," he replied. "You speak very good English for a Frenchman, Chevalier."

"Ah," said Truthful hastily. "My cousins are English, and I had an English tutor. I have always studied most diligently, sir."

"I can believe it," said Harnett dryly. "You certainly can't box. You should visit Gentleman Jackson and learn a little science if you stay long in England. Your cousins will take you, I'm sure."

"They are both ladies," replied Truthful. Remembering her story, she added, "I have no partiality for sparring or sport of any kind. I am to become a monk."

"No!" cried the Major, quite taken aback. "That's infamous! You're a young gamecock if ever I saw one. You should be cutting a spree, not moldering in religion!"

"That is what Father says," sighed Truthful, playing her role to the full. "But I have always desired solitude and quiet contemplation. . . ."

"Hold hard!" cried Harnett. "How old are you, boy?"

"Nineteen," replied Truthful.

"I was with the Ninety-Fifth in Spain when I was nineteen," mused Harnett, shaking his head sorrowfully. Truthful smiled to herself as she realized he was thinking of her as what her cousins would call "a regular green 'un."

"Well, there's not too much harm done," he said, thrusting out a hand and smiling engagingly. "I daresay I've sometimes not looked where I was going."

"You are most kind, sir," replied Truthful, clasping his hand with what she hoped was a manly gesture. But as they touched, a spark of something shot through her arm. She gripped his fingers lightly and couldn't meet his eye.

"Perhaps, Major," she said, hastily letting go, "you could direct me as to how I might find my way from here to Grosvenor Square."

"Grosvenor Square?" said Harnett, raising an eyebrow. "Who are your cousins?"

"I am staying with Lady Badgery," replied Truthful, "and my cousin, her great-niece, who is Lady Truthful Newington."

"Don't know either of them," said Harnett. "I don't go out in society much these days. Newington? There's an old buzzard of an Admiral by that name...."

"He is not an old buzzard!" exclaimed Truthful angrily. "He is my . . . my cousin also! I am not surprised you do not go about in society, if that is how you speak of respectable people!"

"I mean no harm," replied the major with surprise. "You've a very womanish sensibility, my boy, if that sort of talk offends. I daresay you've yet to see the insides of Cribb's Parlour, or a hell—"

"And I do not intend to," snapped Truthful. "Now, sir, if you will direct me to Grosvenor Square!"

"Of course," replied the major. "Of course . . . Newington . . . Newington. There was something else about the name, some on-dit about town, I heard yesterday. . . ."

"Oh!" cried Truthful. She forgot to be angry, her voice going high. She continued more gruffly, trying not to show her eagerness to find out what people were saying about her. "Please, tell me what it was?"

"I should have recalled it earlier," mused the Major, stepping back and looking Truthful up and down as she blushed hotly and clenched her fists. "Yes, I should have indeed, with the evidence in front of me! As I said, Chevalier, I infrequently visit London, and am not sociable at all. But last night I came to town to dine with friends, and I heard a curious story about an heiress who has come to London in search of a lost gem, and since she cannot actively search for it herself, employs her French cousin to do so on her behalf. A womanish sort of cousin, I am told, who is excessively quiet and pious. Hardly the sort of fellow one employs in such a serious affair, even if you are due more credit than the tale tells."

"Lady Troutbridge!" hissed Truthful, wishing that whatever sickness had slowed her gossip would return threefold. Then, louder, she said, "Lady Truthful had no one else to turn to, sir. But it is true that I am not practiced in these matters."

"Have you talked to someone who is?" asked Harnett, and Truthful saw that he was quite serious. He wasn't mocking her.

"*Non,*" she replied despondently. "I know so few people in London. My friends are all abroad. It is impossible."

"There is one man you should definitely consult," said Harnett. "In fact, I shall be taking supper with him tonight at White's. I think you should accompany me."

"White's!" exclaimed Truthful, thinking of that solid male bastion, its many highly sorcerous members, and the potential fragility of her glamour. "But I am not a member!"

"In that case, we shall both be guests of General Leye," said Major Harnett. "He is just the man to help you and Lady Truthful find your lost jewel."

Truthful looked at him cautiously. He seemed friendly enough now, and his air of easy competence was comforting. But he could represent a danger to Lady Truthful, at the very least. An unknown, sold-out major who dressed in such a slipshod fashion (even in a backstreet) might well be a fortune hunter of some kind. He certainly looked like he needed money. He freely admitted to not going about in society, and he wasn't a member of White's. Evidently he was not a man of the first stare. But if he knew General Leye, as he claimed . . .

Truthful had heard a great deal about *him*, for General Leye had been the premier spy-catcher of the long wars against Napoleon, and must certainly have the sort of inquisitive mind and experience that would greatly aid her search for the Emerald.

"I must accept," she said finally. "Truly, I need help. At what hour, Major?"

"Oh, ten at the club," replied the major. "I'd give you my card, but I've left my case in my coat. Just ask for General Leye. We'll be in a private supper room, of course. There's no need to tell Lady Truthful about this. Best to keep the womenfolk in the dark on the details. Tell 'em you're out with friends."

"Of course," replied Truthful, the faintest smile twitching her lips. They shook hands again, she mounted to ride away, hesitated, and both said, "Directions!"

Harnett gave her the directions she required without condescension and watched her walk her horse to the corner and advance into a trot. As she disappeared out of sight, two other men sauntered out of doorways nearby. One was the watchman who'd given Truthful the earlier directions that had led her to the lane, and the other was a man dressed much like Harnett, if a little more stained with ink.

"An interesting method of introduction," the latter said as he strolled across. "But I wish you hadn't used my manuscript."

"I had to look like I belonged in this inky little street," replied the "major." "I'm afraid I've had to appropriate your name as well; the Frenchman saw the title page. I'm glad you were here, Harnett. I've been following him all morning without the chance of concocting an accidental meeting."

"Thank you for your part, too, Sergeant Ruggins," he added to the watchman, who was standing at attention next to the real Harnett.

"I don't know why I oblige you, Charles," said Harnett, taking his manuscript and looking at it sadly. "Heaven knows why I do, considering the scrapes you've got me into."

"My natural charm," said Charles, who had turned back to look out the way Truthful departed. "There's something dashed peculiar about that Frenchman, James. A whiff of sorcery of some kind. I can't quite fathom it yet, but I'm glad the general asked me to look into the fellow. Bonaparte still has his supporters, both in and out of France, and despite everything the Sorcerer-Royal says publicly, apparently it might be possible to release him from his immurement within the Rock."

"Surely not!" protested Harnett. He had been present at the ceremony in Gibraltar himself when the former emperor of the French was sorcerously imprisoned deep within the massive rock that guarded the passage between the Mediterranean and the Atlantic.

"So Ned says," replied Charles. "And as always, he would know. And if Boney does get free, he'll have an army of two hundred thousand Frenchmen within a week. It'll be the Hundred Days all over again, with us even less prepared than last time. Curse the French!"

"Cloak and dagger," muttered Harnett, shaking his head, though he knew in the case of his old friend that it was not merely the war that had turned him against France and her people. "You and the general have been in your twilight world too long, Charles. I'll wager you haven't even told your uncle and aunt you're back in England."

"True enough," replied Charles, taking him by the arm and leading him back through the doorway. "But I am planning to retire after this matter of the Frenchman and the Newington Emerald. Now, tell me what you know about Lady Truthful Newington. Is she as beautiful as they say, or merely rich and spoiled?"

"All three, I suspect," replied Harnett. "Haven't met her. Duckmanton saw her in the park, and declares her ravishing but over-proud."

Sergeant Ruggins, closing the door after the two gentlemen, heard his superior laugh and caught the words "Duckmanton . . . aground . . . heiress" and then "mooncalf" before the door slammed and their voices were lost in the grinding of the key in the iron lock.

SUPPER AT WHITE'S

*T*ruthful returned to Lady Badgery's house in the guise of the Chevalier de Vienne, made a brief reappearance in her feminine guise to announce that she had a sick headache and would not be attending a planned card party that night, then devoted herself to preparing her evening costume for the appearance of de Vienne at White's.

Fortunately, or perhaps shockingly (though Truthful innocently thought of it as merely another of her great-aunt's eccentricities), Lady Badgery's house had numerous secret passages. Truthful's bedroom had a hidden door in the wardrobe, leading to a passage that communicated with both a lesser saloon and one of the guest bedrooms on the other side of the house, now given over to the Chevalier de Vienne. So it was quite easy for Lady Truthful Newington to enter her room, a cold compress against her forehead, lock the door behind her, and reappear as the Chevalier de Vienne an hour later, from an entirely different room.

Contrary to the instructions of the man Truthful knew as Major Harnett, Truthful stopped at Lady Badgery's parlor before she went out. After knocking and announcing herself in her male identity, she entered to find Lady Badgery examining a music box cleverly inlaid with mother-of-pearl in the shape of tiny harpsichord keys.

"Ah, my dear boy," said Lady Badgery. She put the box down as Truthful entered, and tilted her head to listen to the delicate air it slowly picked out, winding its way down to a tuneless murmur. "Or perhaps I should say, young man. You are obviously going out this evening."

"Yes, cousin," replied Truthful gruffly, casting a look at one of the maids, who was putting a glass and a bottle of ratafia on the satinwood side table.

"Eliza, please go and fetch some port for the chevalier," said Lady Badgery, smoothly catching Truthful's conspiratorial gaze. "Dworkin will instruct you."

"Yes, milady," replied the maid, bobbing her head to both Lady Badgery and the elegant young Frenchman as she hurried from the room.

"I take it that you have finally found some clue, some indication of the whereabouts of the Emerald?" asked Lady Badgery, gesturing to Truthful to sit down beside her.

"I'm afraid not," said Truthful with a heartfelt sigh. "But I accidentally met a man today, a Major Harnett, who had heard about the loss of the Emerald, probably from—"

"The odious Lady Troutbridge," interrupted Lady Badgery. She slapped the table, making the music box jump and jangle. "She arrived in town the day before yesterday, and has lost no time in spreading that tale. Parkins told me this afternoon."

"Major Harnett said he'd heard it last night, but he didn't say where," exclaimed Truthful. "Then he suggested that I should consult with someone who is expert in these affairs. General Leye. And he invited me to join them both at White's tonight for supper."

"Ned Leye . . ." said Lady Badgery. She frowned and scratched the bridge of her significant nose. "I did consider consulting him. You will have to be careful, my chevalier. He is a very accomplished sorcerer, and has a reputation for seeing through enchantments and glamours. It would mean ruin for Lady Truthful if a certain albeit necessary deception were to be discovered."

"I know," replied Truthful, her elegant white hands

briefly clasped in anxiety. "But I really do need help. If General Leye is as clever as everyone thinks he is, I'm sure he can help me find the Emerald. My . . . my reputation, or lack of it, is of no consequence."

"It is of every consequence!" snapped Lady Badgery. "However—"

A knock on the door interrupted any further conversation, but instead of Eliza, Agatha entered, carrying a tray with a decanter of port and several glasses.

"Where is Eliza?" asked Lady Badgery, who was not fond of her great-niece's cantankerous maid. "And why aren't you attending Lady Truthful?"

"Eliza was suddenly taken ill, milady," replied Agatha. "And Lady Truthful has gone to bed with a headache. Will that be all, milady?"

"Yes, Agatha," said the Dowager Countess, waving her hand to dismiss her. "Please ask Parkins to look after Eliza, and call Dr. Embury if she needs attention."

Agatha nodded and mumbled something appropriate as she turned to go. As her head bent, Truthful noticed that her expression was quite twisted, as if a secret, hidden visage of malice had come to the surface for a moment. Then, as she straightened up and went to the door, it was the old Agatha again, grumbling and cantankerous but with no trace of that cold and cunning look that had flashed across her face the moment before. It had happened so quickly that Truthful wondered if she had imagined that sudden grimace.

"You may take my carriage, of course," said Lady Badgery after Agatha had shut the door. "It wouldn't do to ride up to White's. And do come and tell me all about it when you get home. Even if it's late . . . or early."

"I will," said Truthful, smiling.

"Good," replied the dowager. "I am sure I will get a much more accurate picture of White's from you than I ever have had from my, shall we say, more masculine friends."

"You can be certain of an accurate tale, cousin," laughed Truthful. She sprang out of her chair and bowed low over her great-aunt's proffered hand, enjoying the freedom of pantaloons over her usual cumbersome dress, despite a feeling that it was quite improper to do so.

Shortly before ten o'clock she stepped down from her great-aunt's carriage outside the bow windows of White's, where the famous glamourists Brummel, Alvanley, Mildmay, and Pierrepoint had once lounged and made disparaging comments about passersby. Truthful didn't look toward the window, however, in case she saw someone making just such a disparaging comment about her, or rather, the Chevalier de Vienne. Instead, she walked swiftly up the steps, the porter only just opening the door quickly enough.

The majordomo inside, seeing a face unknown to him,

quickly came forward to ask if he could be of any assistance and to politely eject this young sprig if he was not a member or invited guest.

"I am a guest of General Leye's, monsieur," said Truthful, trying to be at her gruffest and most French. "I am the Chevalier de Vienne."

The majordomo smiled and bowed his head, crooking his finger at the same time to summon a waiting footman to take Truthful's hat and gloves. "James, the chevalier will be joining General Leye's supper party."

Two minutes later, Truthful was standing outside a heavy door deep inside the club. She had caught a quick glimpse of some sort of gaming room as they had traversed a corridor; heard snatches of laughter, talk, and the click of dice and chink of glasses; and smelled several whiffs of smoke from cigars; then they had passed on from the better-known parts of the club toward a private dining room.

The door was opened by Major Harnett, and the footman announced, "The Chevalier de Vienne, sir, to dine with the general."

"Come in, sir!"

Truthful walked in slowly and saw that the room was quite small and dark. There were only a half-dozen candles burning in a tarnished silver-gilt candelabra set on a corner table. In the soft light she saw a portly, balding gentleman with a prominent nose and bushy eyebrows, his tall form resting in a leather armchair rather like a folded-up vulture. She knew him at once from the famous caricature by Thomas Rowlandson, published at the height of Leye's success as a spy-catcher in 1815, shortly before Napoleon's defeat at Waterloo and his subsequent immurement in the Rock of Gibraltar.

"Bonsoir, Chevalier," he said. *"Je suis heureux que vous ayez pu vous joindre à moi ce soir. Vous avez déjà rencontré . . . Major Harnett, je crois?"*[3]

"Oui. Major Harnett et j'ai rencontré ce matin,"[4] replied Truthful carefully, as Harnett stepped toward her from behind the general's chair and inclined his head. The general's French was very fast and fluent, but she had managed to follow it without difficulty. She cast a glance at Harnett as she spoke, partly to see if he had understood the general's French, and partly to admire his dress—although she told herself it was merely for the purpose of furthering her own disguise.

For the ink-stained coatless ruffian of that morning had been replaced by an expensive elegance that stopped short of dandyism. From his astonishingly white knee breeches to

---

3   "Good evening, Chevalier. I'm glad you could join me tonight. You've
     already met Major Harnett, I believe?"

4   "Yes, I do. Major Harnett and I met this morning."

his cravat tied in the waterfall mode, he was attired as a man of taste and consequence. Even his jet-black hair had succumbed to order, swept back in a style Truthful could only admire without recognizing it as being done in the fashion known as à la Brutus.

Supper was a simple affair of white soup, cold meats, poached salmon, curiously cut vegetables that Truthful wondered were some sort of private joke, and various cakes and trifles. But neither the general nor Harnett ate very much, and Truthful followed their example, though she did not do so when it came to drinking the port, for they put away a surprising number of glasses of the wine. Though she knew she drank considerably less than would be usual for most young men of her class she hoped her supposed asceticism and devotion to religion would be sufficient to explain her abstinence.

The initial talk was inconsequential, mostly of the sporting variety, the kind of conversation Truthful was used to overhearing from her cousins. Nevertheless, she listened carefully, not least so she could relay some of it back to her great-aunt. She also learned two small but useful facts. One was that Harnett's first name was Charles, and the other, that he was very much a confidant of General Leye, and furthermore was even known to that still more famous general, the Duke of Wellington. So he was a man of some standing after all, which made it curious that he was not a member of White's.

After dinner, the two men lit cigars, Truthful declining both a cigar and the offer of snuff. She would have liked to try the snuff, for she had heard of several women of great *ton* who took snuff like men, but she feared her inexperience with it would be too telling, even in a Frenchman destined for the priesthood. She did, however, accept a brandy as they moved from the table to the chairs set around a fire, newly kindled by the servant who had just finished laboring with his bellows. But even with the fire lit, there was no great increase of light in the room, particularly as two of the six candles on the side table had gone out.

"Now," said the general as the servant left the room, "we shall get down to business. Which is, I understand, the theft of the Newington Emerald. Perhaps you could tell us all you know, Chevalier."

"Lady Truthful has described to me everything that happened in great detail," said Truthful. "I shall relay it as she told it to me, if you are agreeable."

Both men indicating their assent, Truthful told them the whole story, from the arrival of the Newington-Lacys up to the arrival of "Lady Truthful" in London, with occasional interruptions as the general asked questions or wanted her to elaborate on what she had said.

Truthful concluded her tale by saying that it was a fortunate circumstance that he had arrived in time to take up inquiries for Lady Truthful, in the absence of any other male relatives.

"Very fortunate," said General Leye dryly. He raised a silver-cased eyeglass and looked at Truthful with his great eyebrows wrinkled together. She paled as he stared at her. He blinked, let the monocle fall into his open hand, and glanced at Major Harnett. His brow cleared and the corner of his mouth quirked into a faint smile, there and gone so quickly that Truthful was unsure whether she'd seen it happen. On balance, she thought she had seen it, and General Leye had seen something too. But the smile gave her hope.

"It is fortunate, too," he added, "that Lady Badgery is a woman of great resource, not to mention a very fine *sorceress*."

"What I don't understand," said Harnett, oblivious to this sally, "is these Newington-Lacy cousins. Why head off to secure a replacement gem instead of searching for the stolen one? Their leaving looks suspicious in the extreme."

"Adventure!" interrupted the general. "Remember when you were under twenty, Charles? Any excuse to escape to adventure was welcome. Why, you took it yourself, joining the colors."

"Oh," said Truthful, suddenly seeing her cousins'

eagerness to help as less unselfish concern and more simple high spirits. Or indeed, the effect of spirits . . . she hadn't mentioned the rum punch to the general and Major Harnett.

"Not that it doesn't do them credit," said General Leye. "Brave lads. But they didn't think it through. Neither did Lady Truthful. Now, we rule out the cloud-catcher or smoke-devil. Nothing of that sort could even touch an *objet de puissance* like the Emerald! That would have been a bit of misdirection from someone. Easy enough to swirl a bit of cloud about, don't need much talent or power for that. No, there has to be a human agency at work and, as always, I suspect a fairly obvious one."

"An obvious one . . ." said Truthful, her voice faltering.

"Lady Truthful has been too trusting. I fear she suffers from a blindness common in the well-bred. Plain as the nose on your face."

"Blindness," mused Harnett, a lock of his dark hair escaping to fall across his brooding forehead. "Yes, yes . . . I see."

"You mean you know what happened to the Emerald?" asked Truthful. "After simply hearing my, that is, my version of Lady Truthful's story?"

"I have a very good suspicion that must be tested," said the general, leaning toward the fireplace to firmly stub out his cigar on the head of a bronze firedog. He settled back in his chair and said, "Those of higher rank do tend to forget the servants, both for good and ill. Too used to paying them no mind. Not sensible, for many reasons."

"You mean . . ." faltered Truthful.

"The maid. Agatha. Only possible person. Don't believe anyone else could have entered in the short space of darkness. The Emerald was knocked to the floor when the table went over. It must have been picked up when Agatha brought the lamp in. I expect she curtsied, did some bent-over truckling or something similar?"

"Agatha!" said Truthful, stunned. In hindsight, it was obvious, of course, once the magical intervention was discounted. The dropping of the smelling salts, her voluminous dress billowing out as she knelt, covering the Emerald so she could pick it up with her left hand while fetching the smelling salts with her right.

"But Agatha has been . . . Lady Truthful's maid since before she was twelve! Seven years!" she exclaimed. "What could she do with the Emerald anyway?"

"Certainly couldn't sell it," replied the general, reaching across to pour himself another brandy from the decanter on the side table. "She would be very unlikely to have the contacts of a proper jewel thief. She probably stole it for someone else. Given the Emerald's properties, it's more than possible she had been waiting to steal it for seven years. Who did she work for before she came to Lady Truthful, d'ye know?"

"No," said Truthful, who really didn't know. A second later, she realized that would be the only possible answer the chevalier could give. Looking back at the general, she saw the twinkle in his eye again, and with a sinking heart she knew that he had penetrated her disguise, but wouldn't give her away if she were clever enough to keep up the deception. Harnett didn't appear to have noticed, and the general was enjoying pulling the wool over his young colleague's eyes.

"Pity," said the general. "I would investigate this Agatha closely, and her past employers. Is she still with Lady Truthful? She hasn't run away, or disappeared?"

"No, she is still there," replied Truthful, thinking back to the last time she'd seen Agatha, and her surprise entrance into Lady Badgery's room. Had she been listening at the door? Probably, she decided as she thought back over the years of their association. Agatha had never been close to her, not like Parkins was to Lady Badgery. Strange, thought Truthful, that this had never crossed her mind before. Agatha had always been there, cantankerous and difficult, though generally efficient. But she had never shown any kindness or given the slightest hint of affection. Now, as Truthful thought of just how much Agatha had been an accepted part of the background of her life, she realized she knew very little about the maid, her true character, or her private life. Or what she might have been before she came to look after a little girl of twelve. Her father would have hired Agatha in the first place, but the Admiral was not one to look deeply into the matter of domestic staff. It was likely he hadn't even checked her references, taking whatever letters Agatha had brought with her at face value.

"I suggest that she be questioned immediately," continued the general. "I am sure Major Harnett will be willing to assist you."

"Certainly!" exclaimed Harnett, as if he had been waiting for his cue. "I shall be delighted. To tell the truth, I shall welcome an opportunity to meet Lady Truthful, if all that is said about her beauty is true. Mind you, most recognized beauties have too much pride and ice bound up in their looks. I daresay Lady Truthful's just another of those! What do you think, de Vienne?"

"I don't believe so," replied Truthful, her back stiffening. Was she a proud beauty? Were people really talking about her like that?

"I heard she cut Trellingsworth in the Park the other day," continued Harnett. "Cut the poor fellow dead. Just acted as if she hadn't seen him. I mean, Trellingsworth is a fool, but to cut him like that! The man won't recover for a week. She must be the very devil for haughtiness."

"Now, now, Charles," said the general, seeing Truthful

staring at Charles as if she was about to either burst into tears or brain him with the poker. "You've embarrassed the poor chap. Remember Lady Truthful is his cousin!"

"What's that matter?" asked Charles. "My sister's an out-and-out harpy and I'm the first to admit it."

"Perhaps Lady Truthful really didn't see Mr. Trellingsworth," said Truthful, which was, in fact, the case. "The Park is full of trees, and Mr. Trellingsworth does tend to wear a very, very disguising shade of green."

Charles opened his mouth to answer, but the general smoothly interrupted before he could begin.

"You probably don't know it, de Vienne, but Charles is well known for his rather jaundiced opinion on the fairer sex, unfairly basing his view of all of them on the actions of one."

"I have yet to see evidence that I am wrong," said Charles stiffly. "Furthermore, let me say—"

"No. This isn't the time for you to make commentaries on young ladies, Charles. I suggest you go and tell Westingham to bring de Vienne's carriage around, and you can accompany him to Grosvenor Square and question this Agatha. No time like the present, I always say."

"But it's almost midnight," protested Truthful. "Surely a commotion at this hour—"

"Best time," interrupted Harnett. "She'll not be expecting

it. You can ask Lady Truthful to call her for some reason, and we'll be waiting to question her. Simple, really."

"But Lady Truthful will be in bed. She retired early with a sick headache."

"I'm sure she won't object if it means we recover the Emerald," interrupted Harnett again. He stood up and rubbed his hands together, with every sign of someone who is about to enjoy a bracing adventure. "I'll go and order the coach, de Vienne. I'll be out in front in a few minutes. General, your servant, sir."

Then he was gone, almost running out the door. Truthful blinked at where he'd been standing a moment before. The general winked at her and chuckled, then burst out into outright laughter before quieting and wiping his eyes with a red silk handkerchief.

"I'm sorry, my dear," he said weakly. "I should not let humor overcome me, for this is really quite a serious matter. The Emerald is a very powerful talisman, and in the wrong hands . . . But fancy Charles not realizing who you are! He told me, 'There's something dashed peculiar about that Frenchman.' Ha-ha!"

He started chuckling again, but subsided as Truthful said primly, "I don't like deceiving people. I had no choice."

"No, no. You're doing very well," replied the general seriously. "I admire your pluck, young lady, not to mention your great-aunt's skill with illusion. Fixed in that mous-tache, ain't it? And Charles isn't all he says he is either, so don't let that distress you. I suppose he never had the ben-efit of knowing your mother, so it's no great surprise that he thinks you are merely an effeminate Frenchman."

"You knew my mother?" asked Truthful, completely distracted. She hardly ever met anyone who had known her mother, and since it upset her father to speak of his dead wife, she had little opportunity to hear anything of that dimly remembered figure. "Oh, I see. I am supposed to resemble her."

"Resemble her!" said the general. "Alike as two peas in a pod, and I can see it even through that glamour and those clothes. But there's few folk around who would remember Venetia when she was young. She married your father soon after she was twenty, and rarely came to London. She never much cared for society, you know. Now, you'd best go and meet Charles and capture your thieving maid. Frankly, I'm surprised she's still there, even if staying would allay suspi-cion. Come and see me as yourself, when it's safely done, my dear—and good luck."

Truthful nodded, clasped her hand in the general's briefly in unspoken thanks, and leaped up. The sooner she could confront Agatha, the sooner she could recover the Emerald—and cease her impersonation, which was beginning to embarrass her, particularly hearing comments about herself from Harnett.

Major Harnett and Truthful had little to say during the short coach ride to Grosvenor Square, though the major did ask her a few questions about the layout of the house, whether the servants' quarters had windows and the proximity of Agatha's room to the kitchen door. Truthful answered vaguely and with some shame, remembering General Leye's words about ignoring servants, for she couldn't provide any details, not having ventured into those regions. She was also distracted by trying to work out how to resume her identity as Lady Truthful, summon Agatha, and then reappear as the Chevalier de Vienne.

Unfortunately, no plan of action occurred to her, and she began to fidget slightly, a symptom of a nervous sort of fear akin to being found out when she had been naughty as a child. However, as the coach pulled up in front of the house and Truthful looked out, she had the feeling of a reprieve. The whole house was lit up as if for a party (but no party had been planned) and she could see shadows moving about both the upper and lower rooms. Obviously, something had happened in her absence, for the entire household was awake.

Awake and in turmoil, as they discovered when they entered the hall. Dworkin, the butler, was directing half-asleep servants to catalog the silver; Lady Badgery's secretary was disappearing into his study with a large tome that Truthful recognized as an inventory; and Lady Badgery herself was standing imperiously on the staircase, Parkins behind her. Truthful knew that she must be very upset, for though she was wearing her favorite fez she made no move to remove it or to retreat when she saw Harnett come in behind Truthful.

"Ah, cousin de Vienne," cried Lady Badgery as she saw them enter. "And this is?"

"Major Harnett, at your service, milady," said the major, doffing his hat and bowing gracefully. "May I be of some assistance?"

Lady Badgery looked him up and down with regal consideration and seemed to approve of what she saw. "You are obviously a man of action, sir, and perceiving action, wish to be a part of it. However, I have already sent a man for the Bow Street Runners, and I fear there is nothing else to be done."

"But what has happened?" cried Truthful.

"Lady Truthful's maid, Agatha," pronounced Lady Badgery, "has drugged poor Eliza and run off, probably with half the silver!"

7

AGATHA'S PREVIOUS EMPLOYER

Eventually, it was discovered that Agatha hadn't taken anything other than her own clothes, and had left no evidence to suggest where she might have gone. Accordingly, several Bow Street Runners immediately lost interest and departed, grumbling about false alarms and rude awakenings. A runaway maid was not of the same importance as a thieving maid and a great quantity of stolen silver, and no one mentioned the Emerald.

By three o'clock that morning, the house had quieted again, leaving Harnett, the ostensible de Vienne, and Lady Badgery having a quiet conference in the drawing room.

Truthful quickly relayed the general's opinion to Lady Badgery, who seemed unsurprised.

"Thought of her myself," she said sourly. "But then I never liked her, so I had to take my natural dislike into account, and she was still with Lady Truthful, which lulled my suspicions. Surely she would have run away as soon as she arrived in London?"

"A clever ploy," replied Harnett. "And a successful one. Perhaps she needed to make some arrangements . . . hmmm . . . we must find out more about this maid. Would it be possible for you to have Lady Truthful woken up, milady?"

Lady Badgery looked at him disapprovingly, as only a dowager could, though her fez somewhat lessened the effect. "At three in the morning? When she has been ill with a sick headache?"

"I think that we must move ahead as quickly as possible," replied the major. "Saving your presence, milady, I know that many sick headaches in ladies are simply nerves. . . ."

He faltered to a stop as Lady Badgery's brow furrowed still further into a definite frown, and a chilly silence spread through the room.

"Perhaps Lady Truthful should be woken up," said Truthful hurriedly, ending with a long and only partly feigned yawn, half smothered by a slow-moving hand. As she yawned, her gaze met her great-aunt's, and she saw a twinkle appear to match that in her own eyes.

"Oh, very well," snapped the dowager. "But I absolutely insist that you go to bed, Chevalier! Why, your mother would not be pleased to see you up so late, with your delicate constitution."

Truthful looked out of the corner of her eye as Lady Badgery continued in this vein, and saw Major Harnett studiously looking at a portrait of the late Lord Badgery in a corner of the room. Harnett's lip was slightly curled, and it was only too obvious he had no great opinion of the Chevalier de Vienne, just as he had earlier voiced no great opinion of Lady Truthful. Well, thought Truthful angrily as she stifled another pathetic yawn, let him have what he expects.

"Yes, you are right, cousin," she said to Lady Badgery. "I shall ask Parkins to wake Lady Truthful on my way up to bed. Good night, Major Harnett. Thank you for your assistance, and for the most interesting supper with General Leye."

"Good night, Chevalier," replied Harnett politely. Truthful wasn't sure if there was a slight note of condescension in his voice, or she just imagined it must be there. "I trust that we shall soon unravel this whole sorry affair."

"I expect so," replied Truthful, smiling. "Good night, cousin."

Forty minutes later, Harnett and Lady Badgery's polite conversation about very little (which had succeeded an unsuccessful attempt by Lady Badgery to discern his ancestry) was interrupted by the querulous voice of a young woman.

"What is going on, Great-aunt? Parkins absolutely insisted I must get up, and I have a quite awful headache! What has Agatha done?"

This speech was rapidly followed by the speaker, a young woman carefully attired in a pale green morning half dress with a white demitrain, gray slippers, and a green and white bonnet. A few ringlets of her red hair escaped from under the latter, artful testimony to a rushed awakening.

"Allow me to present Major Harnett," said Lady Badgery.

"How do you do?" said Truthful coldly. She let her eyes cross the major disdainfully to slide with obvious intent to the clock on the mantelpiece before adding, "I am unused to . . . gentlemen . . . callers at this hour of the morning."

"I am not calling in the usual way," said Harnett, with considerable reserve. "Your cousin, the Chevalier de Vienne, dined with myself and General Leye this evening, hoping to enlist the general's assistance in the search for the Newington Emerald. Your Emerald, Lady Truthful."

"Oh yes?" replied Truthful, pointing one dove gray slipper and looking at it as if it displeased her. "I hope it was an enjoyable evening."

"It was a productive one," said the major, bristling. "The general deduced that the Emerald was stolen by your maid, Agatha."

"La!" cried Truthful, in a show of languid surprise. "The disloyal creature! Father shall have her caned, I expect."

This sally met with silence, and Truthful, looking at Harnett through the corner of one half-lidded eye, felt both unholy glee at playing the spoiled young lady and a strong tinge of guilt that had shades of something else. Did she really want Harnett to detest her, just because he had formed an opinion of her from what he had heard?

"I'm afraid, Lady Truthful, that you will not be able to have Agatha caned or punished in any way unless you can catch her," said Harnett coldly. "The commotion that has kept us up to this hour, and led to your own disturbed rest, was caused by the sudden decamping of your maid. She could be halfway to Dover and a ship by now. With your Emerald."

"Oh," said Truthful, more realistically. She hadn't thought beyond her immediate pleasure in playing the Lady Truthful Harnett expected.

"You suspect she will flee to France?" asked Lady Badgery.

"I believe it is a strong possibility," replied the major. "Certainly, it would be in the best interests of such a criminal to sell the gem in some far corner of the Continent, where its provenance would not be known."

"What can we do?" asked Truthful, almost beseech-ingly, before she remembered her chosen role. "I presume that you will assist a lady in distress, sir?"

Harnett looked at her coldly. "As I am now involved in this matter, Lady Truthful, I could not withdraw even should I wish to do so."

"That was an ungallant speech, Major," interrupted Lady Badgery before he could continue. She moved slightly in between the straight-backed major and the stiff-legged Truthful, like someone intervening between a dog and a cat. "However, my niece and I will be very grateful for your help. What is our first step, may I ask?"

The major turned away from Truthful and bowed to Lady Badgery. "A gallant speech from you, milady, only heightens my lack of courtesy. I apologize to you both."

He turned back to incline his head at Truthful, and for a second their eyes met. She saw a glint of anger there, as if he didn't really want to apologize to her, and she felt her own eyes sparking anger back. With the fleeting thought that she might regret it, she cast herself even more into her playacting.

"Oh, I regard such things as words little, Major," she replied archly. "I judge a man by his actions. One always hears so much mere talk, don't you agree?"

"As you say, Lady Truthful," said Harnett, neatly turning her insult. "We must begin with words, however. For instance, can you tell me who employed Agatha before she came to be your maid?"

"Oh no," laughed Truthful. "I have much more important things to do than inquire where servants come from, why—"

"Parkins will know," interrupted Lady Badgery, casting a daunting glance at Truthful. "She always knows everything there is to know about anyone who comes to this house, family, servants, or visitors."

"Thank you, milady," said Harnett. He coughed and pulled a watch from his waistcoat, the silver chain tinkling slightly. "I think it might after all be best if I return later in the morning to speak to Parkins. I shall then make myself available for the whole day, if any concrete evidence should come forward."

"That is most kind," replied Lady Badgery. "I am sure that the chevalier will be delighted to assist you."

Major Harnett nodded without enthusiasm, bowed again to Lady Badgery, and then, rather perfunctorily, to Truthful. As he straightened up, she felt a twinge of remorse, and held out her hand, saying in her normal tones, "I . . . I do thank you, Major."

He merely touched her fingers, and his reply seemed to be directed at someone rather taller than her who was standing several feet behind.

"I look upon it as a necessary duty, Lady Truthful. I shall recover the Emerald for you. Good night."

With that, he turned on his heel and left. Through the parlor door, Truthful saw him storm down the stair to the front door, snatching his hat and gloves from Dworkin, who was coming up to meet him.

"You were very rude, child," said Lady Badgery. "He is helping you, you know."

"I know," said Truthful despondently. "But he said that I was haughty and icy, and cut poor Mr. Trellingsworth on purpose. . . ."

"And now you have confirmed his opinion," sighed Lady Badgery. "With a dose of silliness added to the haughtiness and ice. Fortunately, he is not someone of the first rank. I have never heard of the Harnetts of Yorkshire. It is odd, for his manners and bearing. . . . It is not important."

She looked around to make sure they were alone, then bent down to Truthful's ear. "You had best go to bed, Truthful. For Henri will doubtless be called early, if this Harnett is the sort of man I suspect."

"Good night, Great-aunt," sighed Truthful, kissing Lady Badgery lightly on the cheek. "And I thank you, at least, for your efforts on my behalf. Oh . . . I wish Father had never shown me the Emerald!"

❦

The morning did begin early, as Lady Badgery had predicted. Major Harnett was at the house soon after eight, and Truthful had to stick on her moustache and appear as the Chevalier de Vienne while Harnett waited to question Parkins, as Lady Badgery had decided to question Parkins herself first. What she heard resulted in a screech of outrage from the old lady that brought Truthful rushing to her bedroom. Parkins and Dworkin were standing by the foot of the bed, both seemingly untroubled by the old lady shrieking and tearing at the sheets.

"Lady Amelia Plathenden!" she hissed after another series of anger-venting shrieks. "That viper! Vixen! I see it now, a long plot and one worthy of that poisonous woman. Why, I'll—"

Seeing her niece staring at her from the doorway, she calmed herself and took several deep breaths. "I must be growing old, not to think of Amelia Plathenden! Where is Major Harnett?"

"The major is waiting in the library, milady," replied Dworkin. "Perhaps I should fetch you a cordial . . . something calming?"

"No, no," said Lady Badgery testily. "Fetch the major, or

I'll have to explain this whole thing twice. Don't look star-tled, Chevalier, I'm an old woman, and this is a sickroom at the moment, not a bedchamber. Besides, I'm sure Major Harnett has seen many a lady's bedroom in his time."

"Great-aunt!" cried Truthful, genuinely shocked, and then she raised her hands to her face and blushed as she realized she'd said "Great-aunt" and not "Cousin." Dworkin, halfway out the door, turned and, seeing Truthful's look of despair, smiled and laid a finger alongside his nose before closing the door behind him.

"Shockin' behavior for a butler," remarked Lady Badgery. "Close your mouth, Truthful, and stop looking surprised. I told you Dworkin always knows what's going on. Besides, he comes from a long line of witches. I daresay he could see through any glamour of mine."

"Oh," said Truthful. She sat down on the chair next to the bed, then stood up again to spread her coattails for a sec-ond attempt. "I thought I was doing rather well."

"You are, dear," said Lady Badgery. "But even the best glamour can only work for a short time in a house such as this, when you are under close inspection. Some of the other servants may well know or at least suspect. Perhaps Agatha did too. But none of my people will talk . . . or if they do—"

A knock on the door interrupted her, and Truthful got up to let Harnett in. As he passed, she couldn't help running

her eyes over him, taking in his sober blue coat, fawn pantaloons, and shining top boots. These, while highly polished,
lacked the glow that rumor said could only be gained by a
mixture of champagne and polish applied by a master valet.
His hair too was only lightly brushed back, a sad remnant of
the style he'd affected the night before, and his face was set
in fairly grim lines. Despite all this, Truthful found that she
would rather look at him than any dandy, and realizing this,
she denied it to herself and looked away. Before the major
could say good morning, Lady Badgery spoke.

"Good morning, Major Harnett. Please be seated. You
too, Chevalier. As you can see, I find myself confined to my
sickbed by the rigors of last night's incident. I apologize.
However, it is fortunate I was lying down, otherwise I suspect I would have suffered a fit of apoplexy when Parkins
told me Agatha was once the personal maid of . . . of Lady
Amelia Plathenden."

A lack of recognition greeted these words, and the old
lady looked somewhat miffed that Truthful and Harnett
hadn't suffered from a fit of apoplexy as well.

"Who is Lady Plathenden?" asked Truthful. "And why
would . . ."

"I'm coming to that! Don't be impatient, young man. The
theft of the Emerald has obviously been a long-planned plot

of the vilest nature, Major Harnett. This became apparent to me as soon as I heard that Agatha used to be Lady Plathenden's maid. You see, Amelia Plathenden was very nearly Amelia Newington."

"What?" cried Truthful, jerking forward in her chair.

"Oh, stop interrupting, Chevalier!" cried Lady Badgery. "Twenty-two years ago, Tancred Newington, the Admiral's oldest brother, was heir to the title and the Emerald. He became engaged to Amelia Corbere, as she then was. However, she was caught in some indiscretion, and Tancred broke the engagement. They argued in public, and Amelia was heard to say that she only wanted to marry him for the Emerald.

"This became only too obvious later, as she then set her cap at George, the middle brother, and then at Edmund, that is, Truthful's father, the Admiral. Neither succumbed to her charms, I'm glad to say.

"Now, as you may know, both Tancred and George died shortly after Edmund married. So there was no legitimate way for Amelia to procure the Emerald—and as it was hidden in a secret location at Newington Hall, little chance of stealing it either. Perhaps Amelia gave up her desire for the Emerald then, only to have that desire rekindled when the opportunity presented itself to put her maid into the household."

"Excuse me, milady," said Harnett slowly. "Are you saying that Lady Plathenden conceived a plan for stealing the Emerald that would take more than seven years to mature? And that she now has the Emerald?"

"Yes and yes!" exclaimed Lady Badgery. "That woman never forgets, and when she wants something, she either gets it or destroys it! Why, I even suspect that George and Tancred didn't die of any common illness. . . ."

Shocked silence met her words, and the old woman seemed to subside a little into the bed.

"There was no proof," she muttered. "Her husband was a malignant sorcerer, and it was long rumored that she practiced dark arts herself and was even twice investigated by the Argent Pursuivant. But no charges were laid, the proof insufficient, or so it was said. But she hated them both, and she danced with Tancred and George at a ball the night before they fell sick. I should have been there, I might have seen it . . . but I was not. They were hearty men, my nephews, but dead within the week. She would have murdered Truthful's father too, I'm sure, but Venetia—Truthful's mother—was wary of her, and she made sure her Edmund was safe from Amelia Plathenden."

"Begging your pardon," said Harnett dubiously, "but this is all rather . . . ahem . . . unproven. Possible murders long ago, unsuccessful investigations of malignant sorcery . . .

and there is no evidence Lady Plathenden is involved in the theft of the Emerald. Are you quite certain . . ."

"I have never been more sure, sir," said Lady Badgery, fixing him with an eye that had been known to quell personages up to and including minor royalty. "I may not have scried it, but my every sense tells me it is true."

"Well we can't expect the law to be of any use," began the major. "I mean, there's no clear evidence of devilment, so we can't expect the Argent Pursuivant to become involved, nor would any magistrate, and without a warrant the Runners will not move. Even General Leye could not act officially unless—"

"Lady Plathenden will have to be convinced returning the Emerald will be in her best interests," interrupted Lady Badgery. "Or it must simply be taken back from her."

"Taken back?" asked Truthful.

"*Stolen* back, I think you mean," said Harnett. "Not something . . ."

He paused, looked at Lady Badgery, then across at the white-faced chevalier. "Oh, hang it all! Why not! I'll do it, Lady Badgery. Sometimes it is best to charge straight up to the guns and over them! Lady Plathenden will find herself facing two very unusual gentlemen callers later today. What do you say, Chevalier?"

Truthful stared at him, her false moustache tickling her

upper lip, and saw his barely contained glee. He was actually looking forward to an undoubtedly hostile and socially extremely difficult encounter with the dangerous-sounding Lady Plathenden, a malignant sorceress who might have poisoned Truthful's two uncles.

"I can see why you're not a member of Whitey's!" she blurted out. Then, as puzzlement clouded his face, she said, "I mean . . . is this . . . oh . . . yes, I will be happy to accompany you, sir."

"That's settled then," pronounced Lady Badgery. "Lady Truthful will be most grateful to you both."

"One would think so," said Harnett dryly. "However, I fear your niece is not terribly concerned with the fate of something she probably accounts a mere bauble, its value and sorcerous properties notwithstanding."

"Hmmmm . . ." replied Lady Badgery. "You must remember that she was suffering a *severe* headache when you met, my dear major. Normally she is very even tempered."

"I look forward to meeting her again," said the major, who clearly meant quite the reverse. "However, I shall recover the Emerald because it pleases you, Lady Badgery."

"You are most kind," said Lady Badgery, smiling as he bowed over her hand and turned to go. "It is so nice to have two such charming young men waiting on an old lady. Now go, and fetch me the Emerald."

As the major turned to the door, Lady Badgery looked at Truthful behind his back and winked in a very low and vulgar fashion. After a moment's thought and an internal shudder, Truthful winked back and followed Harnett out the door.

8

THE TREACHEROUS LADY PLATHENDEN

"The door knocker has been removed," remarked Harnett, carefully surveying Lady Plathenden's house from the curtained window of the hackney. "And the drapes are drawn. Either Lady Plathenden is not in residence, or she desires onlookers to gain that impression."

"It is an odd house for a lady, is it not?" asked Truthful. She smoothed her moustache nervously, concerned the glamour was wearing off. It seemed as if her voice wasn't sounding as low as it had before. She peered through a gap in the curtain and shuddered. The house was Elizabethan, built of very dark brick, and resembled a prison more than anything else. No real lady of quality could possibly want to live in such a grim old mausoleum, particularly as it was in a very unfashionable quarter, on the wrong side of the river, and too close to it, with a part of the house even being built out and over the Thames!

"From what little I have garnered about her she is reputed to be more than slightly mad," replied Harnett. "But I would hazard it is a cunning madness. She must have her reasons for living in a house like this. It is very fortresslike. No windows on the ground floor, the upper windows barred, and a rooftop walkway that would be ideal for a villain with a fowling piece."

He stared at the house for a moment longer, drew the hack's curtains completely closed, and bent down to the floor to pick up a wooden case. Two short-barreled pistols lay nestled on red velvet inside. Despite their fine scrollwork and the faint oil-sheen of careful maintenance, they were obviously made for hard use and had received it, judging from the faint marks of old powder burns and the wear on their timberwork. The major took them out one at a time, loaded them with balls of a noticeably silver hue, primed them, and handed one to Truthful.

"Not dueling pistols by any means, but the triggers are somewhat lighter than a service pistol, so be careful, Chevalier. Short barrels, but they'll throw a ball true for twenty paces."

Truthful had shot with her cousins several times, but she took the pistol with a heart that sank as much as the hand that took the sudden weight.

"I thought we would be remonstrating with her, not engaging in a shooting match," she said nervously.

"A precaution," replied Harnett. He shot his cuffs, momentarily revealing silver spell-breaking bracers on his wrists. "Her husband was a very dangerous man indeed, and if she is a malignant sorceress who has poisoned two men and masterminded a jewel theft then she is not to be trifled with. Never trust a woman, Chevalier. I've yet to meet one that preferred a stand-up fight over slyness and deceit!"

"Really?" asked Truthful. "You have had bad luck, I think."

"Have I?" asked Harnett bleakly. "If you knew . . . in any case, be wary of Lady Plathenden."

With that comment, he opened the door on the far side from the house and stepped down, looking both ways along the street as Truthful stepped down behind him, holding her own pistol like him, low at her side.

There were few people about, and no one seemed interested in them. It was a very quiet street, and many of the houses seemed shuttered or deserted. A dead street, thought Truthful, the worst part of the city—worse even than the slums, where at least there was life. Or so she imagined, for Truthful had never seen a London slum, and her welfare visits to tenant farmers on a neighboring estate less well-managed than her father's had been little more than carefully stage-managed exercises on both sides.

Satisfied that the road was clear, Harnett spoke a few words to their driver. Truthful, her attention on imagined slums, didn't hear what he said, but she heard the driver reply, "Yes, sir, Colonel, sir!"

Turning back, Harnett saw her looking at him, her eyebrow raised. He smiled awkwardly and said, "A courtesy promotion, Chevalier. You will find that drivers would call me general if they thought it would produce a coin."

"Actually," said Truthful, "I was wondering how he knew you were a soldier."

"Probably the bearing," muttered Harnett, pulling his hat down lower over his eyes. "Let's get on, shall we? We'll try the servants' entrance."

The servants' entrance lay at the end of a series of steps and a sunken corridor that ran about halfway along the side of the house. Their boots echoed on the flagstones, and Truthful thought the ground sounded hollow, as if a dark chamber lay beneath this dismal passage—but she dismissed it as a morbid fancy, for she was nervous enough to imagine anything.

Unbidden, pieces of half-remembered stories from

Gothic romances sprang to mind. *The Mystery of Romola*, for example, where the heroine found . . . suddenly, a bell rang inside, startling her back to reality. Harnett had pulled the bell rope indicated by a bronze plate that said DELIVERIES at the back door, but there was no answer. He pulled it again and then knocked vigorously, but there was no response. The house stayed still and silent.

A trial of the knob revealed that the door was locked, but this didn't seem to thwart Major Harnett. He pushed and pulled the door several times, observing the travel, and said, "Not barred. Good. Mmmm . . . You may care to look the other way, Chevalier. I fear that I will have to open this door in a way that may prove disturbing to a gentleman of France and a potential priest."

"Of course," replied Truthful stiffly. She was actually rather interested. Surely he wasn't going to break it down? However, she dutifully turned her back and steeled herself for the sound of smashing wood—but heard only a scraping sound and several clicks. When she turned back, she saw the flash of something metallic being returned to Harnett's pocket, and the door was ajar.

Harnett pushed it open and walked in. Truthful, following close behind, saw his right hand tighten on the pistol he held by his side. She felt a brief urge to take his left hand into her own, but repressed this instantly with a quick memory of his scornful comments about women. That memory made her angry, and the anger fueled her courage.

They advanced cautiously through the kitchen, but it was clearly not in use. Everything was put away, and the cooking range was cold, as was the old-style fire pit that looked as ancient as the house. Harnett ran his finger along the table and looked at it.

"No dust," he said. "This has only been vacated in the last few days."

"Shouldn't we go back?" asked Truthful. "If no one is here, I mean."

"No," replied Harnett. "We must look for any evidence that may indicate Lady Badgery is correct in assuming that Plathenden is responsible for the theft of the Emerald. Sorcerous paraphernalia of a malignant kind, for example. Upstairs!"

Truthful sighed and followed him up the kitchen stairs. But there was no sign of habitation in the upper rooms. All the furniture was under covers, all the cabinets were locked, all the candelabra empty. Harnett looked methodically in every room, then gestured to the main staircase. Truthful sighed again and followed.

But on the next landing, they did hear something—a

muffled laugh or cry that sounded quite familiar to Truthful. It came from behind a door farther along the corridor, to their right.

"Truthful's maid! Agatha!"

Harnett nodded and slid forward. The laughter continued and someone else spoke in low tones, the words unclear. Harnett hesitated before the door for a moment, then flung it open.

It was Agatha laughing, but the laugh died in her throat, turning into a sick sort of whine as Harnett and Truthful entered the room. But there was another woman there who was unfazed by the sudden invasion.

Tall, imperious, and still striking-looking despite her age, Lady Amelia Plathenden set down the book she had been reading aloud, turned to face the intruders, and glared. But neither Truthful nor Harnett noticed her glare because their eyes were caught by the Newington Emerald that shone on her bosom, the jewel sparkling in the light from the dozens of candles burning in the silver candelabras on the table and on the mantelpiece of the room's single fire.

"Who are you, and how dare you enter my house?" demanded Lady Plathenden, her pallid cheeks reddening. "I shall have you thrown out at once. Agatha, the bell!"

"Stop!" cried Harnett, as Agatha moved toward a red plush bell rope. He raised his pistol and pointed it squarely at Lady Plathenden. "My name is Major Harnett, milady, and my companion is the Chevalier de Vienne, cousin of Lady Truthful Newington. We have been charged with the recovery of the Newington Emerald."

Lady Plathenden's eyes narrowed, and she raised her chin disdainfully. "What, pray tell, has that to do with me?"

"You happen to be wearing it," replied the major dryly. "Please take it off and give it to the chevalier. We shall then disturb you no longer."

Lady Plathenden's chin lowered. She took a step forward, faltered, and leaned against the book-lined wall as if she was going to faint. Truthful, stepping forward to catch her, suddenly stopped as the old woman snatched a pitted, evil-looking bone wand from a hidden alcove and levelled it at her. The motion was so fast and unexpected that Truthful had no chance to lift her own pistol.

"Don't raise your hand, my handsome chevalier," hissed Lady Plathenden. "You, Major, place your pistol on the floor!"

Truthful stood completely still, her heart thumping wildly. Though she had little native sorcery, the bone wand emanated a malignancy so powerful she could feel it, power that wanted to be released. She could now well believe that this woman had poisoned her uncles.

"You can only curse one of us," said Harnett calmly. He put his pistol on the table nearby, rather than on the floor.

"Then the other will shoot you."

"Then I shall curse the larger," snapped Lady Plathenden, moving her aim to Harnett. "The effete Frenchman would never shoot a woman. Would you, little one?"

"I would shoot you with a glad heart," replied Truthful slowly. "As will our companions outside. They will charge the house if they hear anything untoward."

Lady Plathenden smiled, but her cold eyes did not alter, nor did the wand move. Truthful had hoped she would look out the window, but the witch did not even look away for a moment.

"Agatha," she said. "Stop ringing. They will have heard. Look out the window. Carefully, you dolt! See if you can see anyone watching the house. Bow Street Runners or the like."

Truthful watched Agatha peer through a gap in the drapes and felt a surge of anger and distress. How had she failed to notice Agatha's treacherous nature before?

"There's a hackney and a driver opposite, milady," Agatha reported. "The curtains are drawn. And there's a man on horseback at the end of the street."

"I shall have to be careful, won't I?" muttered Lady Plathenden, apparently to Truthful, though her eyes never left Harnett. "Perhaps a transformation would serve better than a curse. Equally painful, of course."

Truthful watched her eyes flickering between the two of

them and felt the weight of the pistol in her hand. If only she could raise it swiftly enough, but that terrible wand was as steady as if it were held in a vise. . . .

The shelves behind Lady Plathenden creaked. One entire bookcase swung open and a damp, musty smell rolled out from the dark passage behind it. Lady Plathenden's head turned slightly, and both Truthful and Harnett acted.

Truthful clumsily cocked her pistol, priming powder spilling as she rushed to level it at Lady Plathenden. As she did so, Lady Plathenden released the malevolent force of the wand and Harnett snatched up his own pistol and cocked and fired it in one well-practiced motion.

Two shots and the snakelike hiss of the wand sounded at almost the same time, wreathing the room in gunsmoke and eldritch scintillations. Harnett staggered back as Lady Plathenden shrieked and clutched at her arm. Truthful, throwing the spent pistol aside, picked up a candelabra and dashed forward, waving it in the air.

"You've killed him!" she screamed at Lady Plathenden, who retreated against a bookcase and stared at this suddenly berserk Frenchman.

"No she hasn't!" cried Harnett, drawing himself upright, his waistcoat smoldering in several sections, the silver wires of a protective charm sewn within revealed through many tiny, smoking holes. "Look out!"

Lady Plathenden slipped through the secret door as two very large and roughly dressed men emerged from it and advanced, their fists clenched. Truthful stepped back and raised her candelabra, and Harnett levered himself up next to her. Seeing her worried glance, he grinned and said, "Curse-ward held it. You fight well . . . for a French monk."

"A monk?" said one of the ruffians, lowering his guard. "I'm not crossing no man of the cloth."

"I ain't so particular," grunted the other, fixing his rather piggy eyes on Truthful. "You take the big cove."

"Perhaps we could discuss this," said Harnett, signaling Truthful to retreat. He continued to talk as they backed off toward the door. "No sense in all of us getting knocked about. Why don't you let the . . . er . . . monk go, and I'll take on both of you, one at a time."

"We ain't gentlemen," grunted the piggy ruffian, smacking a meaty fist into an opposite palm. It made a sound rather like a stone dropping into the carp pond back home, thought Truthful, and was probably just as hard.

"And neither is we," said another voice, this time from behind.

Truthful whirled around. There were two more thugs behind them now, and both of them carried long cudgels.

"Back to back!" cried Harnett. "If you have any sorcery, use it now, Chevalier!"

Truthful moved to press her slight back against Harnett's broad one, and raised her fists. One of the thugs moved forward, laughing, and was confounded by a sudden crackling of sparks from the signet ring on Harnett's fist, sparks that set the rogue's hair alight and sent him screaming from the room shouting for water.

But the other three attacked, all at once. There was a hurried exchange of blows, Harnett was borne to the floor by two of the thugs, and Truthful's guard was demonstrated to be merely decorative. Two seconds later, a scientific jab to the chin sent her reeling to the floor. She tried to get up, was hit again, and everything went black.

When she regained consciousness, Truthful awoke to an aching jaw and complete darkness. A few attempts at movement also conveyed to her the fact that she was bound hand and foot, and tied around her middle to some large object. When it groaned and shifted, she realized the object was Harnett, and they were tied back-to-back. A few more foot taps then told her they were in a cupboard, albeit a strange cupboard, with curious rounded walls and a very strong stench of some strong spirit. . . .

"A barrel," husked Harnett as Truthful kept on knocking with her feet. "Once a butt of brandy, judging from the odor. Rather ignominious, I feel."

"What will happen to us?" asked Truthful quietly. She felt herself leaning back against his wide shoulders, and stiffened. Would her great-aunt's glamour continue to hold in the current circumstances? She had a vague recollection that being touched for any length of time had a deleterious effect on most illusions. . . .

"I'm afraid I don't know," replied Harnett. "Fortunately, I did arrange a contingency with the hackney driver and some of my friends, so there will be a rescue in due course. However, the thing with rescues is timing, and we shall just have to hope it comes sooner rather than later. How tight are your bonds?"

Truthful flexed her feet and arms, but found no movement in the rope. Nor could she strain free from Harnett, as there was a rope wound several times around both their waists.

"I can't get free, Major."

There was silence for a moment, then Harnett laughed, and Truthful imagined his smile flashing for a moment in the darkness.

"I think you may now safely call me Charles," he said. "As we have become rather close."

Truthful smiled, and almost started to laugh, before she suddenly stopped and scowled instead. How could Harnett laugh, unless he was very confident his friends would come to the rescue? She could see no happy ending, tied up in the dark, in a barrel that absolutely stank of brandy.

"I suppose you had better call me Henri," said Truthful.

She did laugh then, unable to help herself. It seemed so ridiculous that they should be learning each other's first names while tied up inside a barrel. In fact, everything seemed rather ridiculous. Truthful tried to stop laughing and took in a deep, brandy-laced breath, only to discover to her mortification that her laughter had turned to tears, which she quickly stifled, ending in a series of sniffs.

"Laughter is a strong weapon against fear, Chevalier," said Harnett. "But I think none the worse of manly tears."

Truthful almost interrupted to ask how he felt about womanly tears, but managed not to speak. She felt very light-headed and wondered what on earth was wrong with her. Besides being trapped in a barrel, of course.

"I knew a man who wept like a baby before every battle in the Peninsula, but there were none braver," continued Harnett.

"What happened to him?" asked Truthful.

"He was killed at Waterloo," replied Harnett. "So many were. But we're still alive . . . and where there's life, there's . . . um . . . how does that go? I confess to feeling a little astray, I suppose the fumes—"

He stopped speaking suddenly as they heard footsteps

approaching. The footsteps stopped near them, and they heard the cold voice of Lady Plathenden.

"Take this barrel out to the *Undine*," she said. "Tell Captain Fontaine that he is to throw it overboard mid-channel, without looking inside."

"But it isn't sealed," protested a male voice. Truthful recognized the sensitive, religious-minded thug. "It'll sink. I don't hold with drowning, ma'am, it's an ugly way to die. Even for kittens, let alone—"

"Silence! See to it at once, and make sure Fontaine understands exactly what he is to do."

Her footsteps receded, and the barrel suddenly lurched, leaned in balance for a moment, and then crashed on its side. Shaken, Harnett and Truthful braced their legs against the sides, and managed to stay reasonably steady as the barrel rolled, bumping over an uneven floor.

A few minutes later, they heard a heavy door open, the rush of the Thames beyond it, and the creaking of a wharf. More footsteps echoed on the stone, and they felt the barrel being lifted. The carter's feet clattered out onto the wharf, there was a thud as the barrel was dropped a few inches, and then they felt the tell-tale sway of a ship or boat.

"So," said a scornful, French-accented man. "Another one of milady's presents to Neptune? Make it fast on deck—there's no room in the hold. And secure the pigeon loft, you fool!"

"No room at the inn," chortled Harnett. For some reason Truthful found this incredibly funny. In an instant, they were both laughing.

"Stop that!" shouted the voice outside, his words accompanied by a strong kicking administered to the barrel.

This seemed funnier still. Truthful couldn't stop giggling, and Harnett brayed like a donkey.

"I said stop!" said the voice again, followed by several more violent kicks. "Or I'll drown you now!"

Slowly their laughter ebbed away. Truthful yawned and wriggled against the ropes.

"I think I'm ready to be rescued," she said. "Any time now."

There was no answer from Harnett, but Truthful was strangely unalarmed. She felt so tired. Nothing mattered except letting her eyelids continue their slow drift toward complete closure.

She let them close, and fell asleep.

ALL AT SEA

*T*ruthful woke with a start as she felt her stomach climbing up into her mouth, stopping just short in her throat. A wave of giddiness swept through her, and for a second she was disoriented, then the pain in her wrists and ankles reminded her of the ropes, and she felt Harnett's back against her own.

"How . . . long have I been asleep?" she whispered, screwing up her eyes against the faint rays of light that were sneaking through the uncaulked lid of the barrel. She felt absolutely terrible. Her throat was parched and sandpapery, and her stomach very uneasy. "How did I fall asleep?"

"I think three or four hours, perhaps even more," replied Harnett, in a hoarse whisper. "I've been asleep too. There was more than a little brandy left in the bottom of this cask, we were mazed by the fumes. But there's a wind blowing out there now. You can feel it through the cracks, and it's cleansed the air in here. Mind you, I've the devil of a hangover."

"So have I . . . I think," said Truthful, a dull throbbing in her head coming in to join the dryness of her throat. "I've never had one before."

"Bad time to start," muttered Harnett. "I think we must already be entering the Thames Estuary, judging from the swell. They've got a fair wind to carry us away too, damn their eyes."

"And it will only strengthen over the day ahead," said Truthful instinctively. She could feel the nature of the wind, deep inside herself. It was steady enough now, but there was more to come.

"How can you tell . . . ah . . . you have weather magic?"

"A little," said Truthful. "It runs in the family."

"Could you do something to slow us down or hold us back?" asked Harnett eagerly. "I am sure my . . . my friends will be in pursuit, but time is of the essence. Could you reverse the wind, perhaps?"

"I have only a little local power," said Truthful regretfully.

"Not enough to turn a sea wind so firmly established."

She could feel the strength of the breeze in her bones, but the sounds of the ship also confirmed it, the heel of the deck and the crack of canvas filling overhead.

"Do you think your friends will be able to rescue us?"

"They'll try," grunted Harnett, who seemed to be engaged in some form of contortionist's exercise. "It depends on whether there was a ship at hand to be commandeered, or if the Navy could be roused to act, if the word was got out quickly enough. But we can't depend on it, I'm afraid. I have a knife in my boot, a *sgian dubh* from a Scottish friend, but I can't reach it. My arms are wrapped right down to the wrists. What about you?"

"I'm only tied around the elbows," replied Truthful. "If I wriggle down a bit, I can move my arms a little."

"Good!" exclaimed Harnett. "Now, if I move my legs back toward you as far as they will go, do you think you could twist around and reach my boot top?"

"I can try," said Truthful determinedly. She felt Harnett twisting his legs around, and started to wriggle around herself, only to pause as there was a sudden loud snapping noise.

"Good God!" cried Harnett. "Was that the rope?"

"Ah, no," muttered Truthful. It was part of her corset, but she wasn't going to tell him that.

"Can you feel my boot top?" asked Harnett. "The hilt of the knife is on the left side, it should come out easily enough."

"I . . . I . . ." faltered Truthful. She didn't want to touch his leg.

Before she could say anything more, the ship plunged more dramatically than it had been, and she heard the crash of a wave breaking against the bow. A second later, spray fell against the barrel, a fine mist coming through the cracks between the staves.

This reminder of their impending drowning overcame the deeply ingrained lessons of modest behavior. Taking a deep breath, Truthful squirmed around, her hands sliding past his knee to the cool leather of his boot top and then to the hilt of the knife. There was a brief struggle, straining every muscle in Truthful's fingers, then it was free and in her lap. But at a cost. Her ensorcelled moustache felt very insecure upon her upper lip. If it fell off, her glamour would go with it, and her disguise would be revealed.

"Well done, lad," whispered Harnett as Truthful gripped the knife between her knees and started sawing at the rope between her wrists. "There's few Englishmen who can handle themselves as well, my religious friend."

Truthful bit her lip. The rather pleasant feeling she got from his praise was more than counterbalanced by two fears. One that they were going to be drowned anyway, and the second that if they were somehow to survive, her deception would be revealed. Harnett would hate her, and her reputation would be ruined. With her thoughts otherwise occupied, Truthful was rather surprised when her hands suddenly came free.

Quickly, she started cutting the rope around their respective waists. It parted quickly. Truthful slid around and cut the ropes from Harnett's hands, then started on her ankles. It was tricky work now, for the ship was cutting diagonally across a heavier swell, and the breeze had increased to an extent that the ship was now running fast with the wind on her quarter. More water was being shipped across the deck, and the barrel was soaked with spray every few minutes.

Concentrating on her cutting, Truthful heard nothing above the wind and crash of waves, but Harnett suddenly craned back and joined his hands to hers to force the knife through the last strand of rope that bound his ankles.

"Quick," he cried, his large, muscular hands pressing down on her slim fingers. "Someone is opening—"

His words were lost in the crash of another wave. Light suddenly flooded the barrel as the lid was flung open, revealing a stormy sky, a towering mast, and sails—and a ring of armed men, the closest of them holding a cutlass, its blade resting on the edge of the barrel.

"Stand up," he said. Truthful recognized his voice as that of the Frenchman she had overheard when they were being loaded aboard the *Undine*. "I see that you have managed to free yourselves."

Blinking, even against the weak light that filtered through the storm clouds, Truthful and Harnett stood gingerly, clutching at the sides of the barrel for support. The Frenchman and his men watched them carefully, their weapons ready. Now that Truthful was on deck, she saw that the sea was not as rough as she had supposed. The breeze was fair for France, and the ship had a good amount of canvas up.

"I am Captain Fontaine," said the man, inclining his head a fraction so that his dark forelock slipped slightly across his brow. But his eyes didn't leave them, and the cutlass only wavered as he changed his footing to allow for the roll and pitch of the ship. There was cruelty in his eyes, Truthful thought, and his voice was harsh.

"Who are you, my barrel-friends?"

"I am Major Harnett of His Britannic Majesty's Ninety-Fifth Regiment of Rifles," replied Harnett slowly, his eyes flickering over the rest of the ship and the men around them. He didn't look at Truthful, who leaned against him as if she wished she could disappear into his shadow.

"And I am the Chevalier de Vienne," said Truthful wretchedly.

"Really?" asked Fontaine, lazily running his eyes up and down her. He reached forward with his left hand and, with one swift motion, neatly ripped off her moustache. It came away so easily that Truthful realized that it had come unstuck with all the water and was already sliding down her upper lip.

As it parted from her skin, the glamour left her.

She saw the men start and Fontaine begin to smile. But it was Harnett's reaction she cared about. Truthful turned to him and felt him flinch as if he had been struck by a bullet. He stared at her, not speaking. She saw disbelief in his eyes, then a growing spark of anger. But he didn't say a word, he just kept staring till she turned away.

"Take the woman to my cabin," snapped Fontaine. "Lash the man to the bowsprit. Let's send him to Neptune slowly, eh?"

The men surged forward. Harnett brandished his little *sgian dubh* and leaped at Fontaine but his legs, cramped and weakened from their imprisonment, failed him and he fell over the side of the barrel. Fontaine laughed and brought the hilt of his cutlass down upon Harnett's head, knocking him senseless.

Truthful shouted and swung a fist wildly at Fontaine, but one of the sailors grabbed her from behind, wrapping his beefy arms around her while his sardine-laden breath blew across the back of her neck, at least until she jerked her head back and smashed him in the nose, a trick she had seen watching a mill when disguised as a boy with the Newington-Lacys. He let go, gasping, but two more sailors pinned her arms and another gripped her around the knees. She struggled violently, but they pushed her against the mast and held her there.

"Take her to my cabin," ordered Fontaine. "I will attend to her later. But she is not to be harmed! Tie her up, but take care not to hurt her, you understand?"

Fontaine's cabin was the main saloon at the stern of the vessel, under the quarterdeck. It was surprisingly clean and neat, not at all like Truthful's expectations of a festering pirate ship. There were several low wooden lockers against the walls, a polished table bolted to the deck in the center of the cabin, and a red plush lounge under the stern windows, which were currently closed against the elements.

The three sailors rapidly tied Truthful's wrists, then tied the other end of the rope to the table leg, carefully checking that there was enough rope to allow Truthful to reach the lounge. They tested this by dragging her there and throwing her on it, ignoring her kicks and attempts to bite.

But after doing so, the three merely grinned and left. Truthful heard the last locking the cabin door behind him, and then their footsteps clattering up the short ladder to the main deck. She lay still for a moment, her head still a little dizzy from the brandy fumes. Even though the motion of the ship had quieted, the slight roll and pitch did not help her head or her stomach.

"I refuse to . . . be . . . sick," muttered the Admiral's daughter, who'd been raised from an early age to sail a dinghy and had often been at sea on her father's yacht, though never with a brandy-fume hangover.

Seasickness pushed aside, she staggered to her feet and lurched across to the table to see how the sailor had tied the rope to the table leg. A quick examination of the knot brought a smile to her face. He had used a trickster's knot, counting on a landlubber (and a woman) being unable to fathom its tortured windings and loops within loops. Truthful undid it in several seconds, humming a sea shanty to herself, a song that Hetherington used to whistle when he went over the ropes of the Admiral's yacht with a younger Truthful, or when they tied knot after knot for the Admiral to inspect.

Both ends of the rope undone, she coiled it on the table and inspected the lockers, searching for a weapon. But the lockers lived up to their name, being firmly shut by keyed bronze locks, and they were made of solid teak, so Truthful found no way to get them open. In any case, she thought, they probably only contained the captain's private supply of food and drink. She turned to the plush couch and, stripping it of cushions, found a storage space below. But it held only clean sheets and blankets.

The last resort was a drawer in the table. It held a sewing kit, with all the usual paraphernalia of buttons, thread, and small needles. But at some time someone had thrust something more useful through the cloth cover of the kit. Truthful drew it out and held it tightly in her hand. A three-inch curved sailmaker's needle was not much of a weapon, but it was better than nothing.

The shutters on the stern windows were closed, but Truthful unfastened one and eased it open. She looked out at the sea below and the white wake of the ship, and for a moment considered climbing out. She was a good swimmer, but there was no knowing how long she had been unconscious or how far they were from land. Besides, there was Harnett. She couldn't escape without him, and in the current swell he would be drowned if he was left tied to the bowsprit for any length of time.

She couldn't defeat Fontaine and all his crew armed only with a sailmaker's needle. Which meant her only real hope was a rescue, from Harnett's friends with or without the assistance of the Navy. However, they would need time to catch up, time that they might not have. The ship was heeled over and sailing fast, confirming from the little she had seen above decks that it was indeed a fast-sailing brig with a good crew, and as Harnett had noted, the wind was fair for the Continent. . . .

Truthful thought for a moment, weighing up the situation. She had the rope she'd been tied up with, a sailmaker's needle, any amount of thread, a number of sheets and blankets . . .

An idea formed in her head, a sailor's notion. She acted on it quickly, opening the drawer and taking out the heaviest thread. She bit off a good section and used it to lash the door shut. It wouldn't hold for long, but every minute would count. Then she took out the sheets and blankets, quickly laid them out on the floor and began to sew them together. She used long, loose stitches with doubled thread for strength, sewing as she had never sewed before, constantly jabbing herself but ignoring both the pain and the splotches of blood that fell upon the cloth.

Shouts above and an even greater inclination of the deck told her that the crew were trimming the sails, perhaps even spreading more to wring out extra speed. That suggested a chase had begun. If only Fontaine stayed on deck for a little longer. Truthful was finished with the sewing. Now she tied the rope that had been used to secure her firmly around the neck of the makeshift sea anchor she had made, and paid it slowly out the stern window before making the rope fast as unobtrusively as possible around the frame.

Bending over to look down, she saw the anchor billow out and fill, larger than she had hoped. But her stitches needed to hold, and the rope must not be cut.

The clatter of footsteps on the ladder made her whip around. The door rattled as someone tried to open it, but for the moment the thread securing it held. Truthful picked up the big needle again, ran to the door, and stood next to it, her hand raised.

RULE, BRITANNIA!

oud swearing accompanied a heavier tug upon the door, which burst open. Fontaine came in angrily, without looking where he was going. Not seeing Truthful tied up on the lounge where he expected her to be, he began to turn— just as she brought the sailmaker's needle down as hard as she could into his shoulder.

Fontaine screeched like a cat, a high-pitched and extremely unpleasant scream. Truthful pulled the needle out and plunged it in again, but before she could attempt a third attack, she was savagely thrown back against the wall, leaving the needle firmly embedded in Fontaine's shoulder.

"I'll kill you, hell-bitch!" he raged, curiously enough in an English that sounded very like one of the London accents Truthful had just begun to know. "Spitfire!"

Truthful staggered away from him, intent on keeping him from seeing the rope to the sea anchor.

"You're not even French!" she exclaimed. "You're just a filthy English turncoat!"

"I am an officer of the Imperial Guard!" shouted Fontaine, lunging at her. Truthful dodged aside and he careered into the wall. "One of the emperor's most trusted men!"

"Turncoat!" taunted Truthful, dodging another attack. "Traitor!"

Fontaine stopped chasing her and drew himself up as much as he could, his head bowed under the low ceiling. He reached inside his coat and drew out a pocket pistol.

"And no gentleman," said Truthful. She did not straighten up, but readied herself to hurl herself down to the deck on the right. The Newington-Lacys had told her this was always the best thing to do if you were about to be shot, as most pistols pulled up and to the right. Only now did she question how they knew this, or whether it was even remotely true.

The sound of the lock being cocked was the most ominous thing Truthful had ever heard. Fontaine's finger curled about the trigger and pulled it back. There was a terribly loud report, a great deal of smoke, and Truthful felt a savage pain in both elbows. But that was from her violent dive to the deck. If she was hit, she hadn't felt it yet. Apparently this was also a possibility, she had been told by the boys, and the thing to do was to keep moving until you *did* notice whatever terrible wound had been inflicted.

She rolled over and sprang up, leaping for the door. Fontaine raced after her, his fingers clawing the back of her coat without purchase as she ran up the ladder and out onto the deck.

Truthful didn't pause, but immediately flung herself on the nearest ratline and began to climb. Below her, Fontaine emerged shouting expletives in a mixture of French and English. Several sailors ran back from the bows and began to climb up the ratlines around the shrouds supporting the main mast, racing Truthful to the top.

But the Admiral's daughter wasn't just climbing to the fighting top, a kind of crow's nest platform. She slid up through the lubber's hole like a rat and kept on climbing till she could reach out to the backstay, the thick cable that supported the mast from the stern. Withdrawing her hands into the sleeves of her coat to protect her skin, she gripped the stay and jumped off, sliding down the rope to the quarterdeck as her pursuers were still climbing up from the deck.

The surprised mate who was steering the ship lunged at her while trying to keep a hold of the wheel, and succeeded in neither action. Truthful evaded his grasp and the wheel spun out of the mate's hand. The ship luffed up into the wind, sails flapping everywhere. It lost most of its way in a matter of minutes, broaching to against the moderate swell.

"Get her!" shouted Fontaine, fairly shrieking now, as Truthful ran around the quarterdeck, swung on another stay, and kicked a sailor back down the ladder to the main deck. At the same time several other officers were shouting orders for all hands on deck to bring the ship back under steerage way, sailors were emerging from below, and then there came the harsh crack of a gun some distance away on the larboard side.

A sloop of war was bearing down on the wallowing *Undine*, the red ensign flying from her mizzenmast, guns run out and fully manned, a scarlet cluster of marines and a throng of armed seamen in her waist ready to board. An officer in a blue coat was standing at the bow, a speaking trumpet at his mouth.

"Prepare to be boarded! Do not offer resistance!"

This order was answered by a hoarse shout that rose seemingly from the figurehead of the ship.

"About time you got here!"

It was Harnett shouting, Truthful realized. He had survived being lashed to the bowsprit. He *hadn't* drowned, though she doubted he was at all comfortable. A wave of relief flowed through her. She stopped running, turned to face her pursuers, and stretched up to her full height with her nose in the air.

"So you are done up, Monsieur Fontaine!" she said haughtily. "Or whatever your real name is. I shall enjoy seeing you hang!"

Fontaine grimaced, anger stark on his face. Reversing his empty pistol, he brought it savagely down on Truthful's head. She felt an intense burst of pain, had a brief cartwheeling vision of deck, sky, and sea, and then all was blackness.

✦ ⸺ ✦

"Henri . . . I mean, Tru . . . damnation, woman, wake up!"

Harnett was still shouting, thought Truthful, as sound once again entered her head, and with the sound, consciousness. Gingerly, she opened her eyes to see a small portrait of herself reflected in Harnett's eyes of the deepest blue. The color of the sea, she thought dreamily, and smiled.

"Thank God!" exclaimed Harnett. Then, as if suddenly struck by the impropriety of staring at her face from three inches away, he jerked back. "That is, about time!"

Truthful gazed at him dumbly. Even through the throbbing pain in her head, she could see his relief of a moment before fade into an almost hostile stiffness. Deep inside, she felt a sudden pain at the loss of the friendly camaraderie she had enjoyed with him when she had been Henri de Vienne.

144

Only then did she become aware that she was lying on an open deck with several blankets expertly wound around her and tucked up to her chin. Masts loomed up into the dark gray fog above, but they were not the *Undine*'s masts. The yards and rigging were too exact, the sails trimmed just so, the deck too clean. Truthful knew instinctively that this was a king's ship.

"Welcome aboard His Majesty's sloop *Lyonesse*," said another voice. Truthful turned her head to see a young Naval officer beaming down at her. "Though I should wish it were in different circumstances, Miss . . . um . . ."

"The lady's name is not to be revealed," snapped Harnett. "Her identity needs to be concealed for reasons of military secrecy, Captain. Hence the now regrettably incomplete disguise."

"Certainly, sir," replied the Naval officer stiffly, his smile wiped from his face. Truthful felt for him, considering that he had rescued them both, and Harnett in particular from being lashed to a bowsprit.

Harnett obviously realized this as well.

"My apologies, Captain. I am short-tempered. Unlike Naval officers, I am not at home up to my neck in seawater."

"I quite understand, sir," replied the commander, unbending a little. "However, I trust I shall be allowed to introduce myself? Richard Boling, at your service, ma'am.

Master and Commander of the *Lyonesse*."

"Delighted," whispered Truthful. Her head ached terribly, and she found it difficult to open her eyes. "Please, what happened? How did you find us?"

"A belated rescue," said Harnett, before Boling could answer. "My . . . ahem . . . associates were suspicious when we didn't emerge from Lady Plathenden's residence. One of them was watching the river. He saw the *Undine* being loaded from the house and alerted General Leye, who in turn sent an urgent message to the admiralty, though unfortunately of course this all took some time. But once the facts were ascertained, things were put in motion, though I can't say exactly how our rescuers caught up with us. Perhaps you could enlarge on that, Captain Boling?"

"We were in the Pool awaiting dispatches to carry to . . . well, westward," continued Commander Boling, taking his cue. "Orders came for us and several other vessels to search for and intercept the *Undine*, on suspicion of having kidnapped two of General Leye's officers. I have to say that she is an uncommonly fast vessel and we might not have caught her if it weren't for the sea anchor and that scuffle around the wheel. I saw the latter through my glass, but was the former also your work, ma'am?"

"Yes," muttered Truthful. "I didn't know what else to do. . . ."

"I am amazed that a young lady might be so . . . so . . . nautically well-informed," said Captain Boling enthusiastically.

"My father is an ad . . . that is to say my father is a Naval . . . I mean I was brought up to have some familiarity with the sea and ships," said Truthful faintly.

"Even so, you have my utmost admiration, ma'am."

"My head?" asked Truthful, freeing one arm from the blanket and gingerly feeling a sore point on the back of her head. She couldn't quite remember what had happened. A fleeting memory of the Newington-Lacys laughing about Robert's loss of memory after falling off a horse went through her mind. She had been giving Fontaine her well-considered opinion and then . . .

"That damned Frenchman!" erupted Harnett, twisting his hands as if he were wringing Fontaine's neck. "Ah, I beg your pardon. That wretched fellow."

"Oh," replied Truthful, still dazed. "He hit us both on the head, then. We must have identical bruises."

Harnett's hand went automatically to the back of his head, to feel his own memento of Fontaine's bludgeoning. But he brought it back down again with obvious willpower.

"I don't begrudge my own bruises," he said sternly. "But he knew you were a woman!"

"Fellow's practically a pirate," muttered Boling. "Probably get a mention if I hang him from the yardarm. But I suppose you will want to take him away, Colonel?"

"Yes, we will," said Harnett. He hesitated, then added in a lower voice that Truthful almost couldn't catch, "The truth is he's a damned traitor, original name of Kellett. We caught him before, during the war, and he got away. He's been slipping about under our noses for the past year or more. The general will be very pleased to lay him by the heels again."

"I hope he *is* hanged," muttered Truthful.

"He will be dealt with appropriately, milady," said Harnett stiffly. "Fortunately he will no longer offer you any . . . his fate will not be your concern."

Truthful hardly heard him, for behind Harnett's words she saw that he was still deeply angry at her deception and probably angrier at himself for being unable to see through it, an anger exacerbated perhaps by the fact that it was she who had enabled their rescuers to catch up while he had been helpless. Major Harnett, one of General Leye's confidential agents, unable to see through a deception perpetrated by a chit hardly out of the schoolroom, aided by a glamour focused on a false moustache! And then to be held fast and half drowned while a mere woman rigged a makeshift sea anchor and grappled with the enemy coxswain!

She also had the sudden insight that his current embarrassment and cold remoteness could easily grow into a real dislike of Lady Truthful. A dislike founded on something more personal and concrete than stories of her cutting Trellingsworth.

"I am sorry I couldn't tell you who . . . that is . . ." she murmured, looking up at Harnett. "I *had* to adopt my disguise—"

"Best we do not discuss this, or any other matter, in public," said Harnett coldly, and Truthful saw the anger she had feared in his eyes. He met her gaze only for a moment, before turning away to look out upon the sea.

"I see," said Truthful. She suddenly felt angry too. The least Harnett could do was listen to her, she thought. After all, if it wasn't for her he would still be tied to the bowsprit, swilling down great drafts of seawater. She looked over to Commander Boling and smiled at him. "I think I need to rest, Captain."

"Of course, ma'am, I shall have you carried to my cabin," she heard Boling say, but it was muffled and far off. Through half-lidded eyes she looked at Harnett, but he would not look at her. Then she heard footsteps, heard a muttered command, and felt hands lifting her, sailors carrying her in the slung blanket like a stretcher, carrying her away to the captain's cabin.

At the last minute Truthful was unable to resist peeking back at Harnett, hoping that he would turn and look at her.

But he didn't. He just kept staring out to sea.

11

THE RETURN OF LADY TRUTHFUL

The *Lyonesse* anchored in the Pool of London soon after
dawn the next morning. Half an hour later Truthful was hustled ashore wrapped up in a boat cloak, a long
woolen muffler, and a rather disreputable broad-brimmed
straw hat that Captain Boling somewhat shamefacedly said
had once been very fine but had suffered from the rigors of a
voyage home from the West Indies.

Truthful did not see Major Harnett, and upon inquiry
was told that he had been met immediately after their
anchoring by several grim-faced officials and a file of sol-
diers in a longboat. They had taken Fontaine away in irons

without waking Truthful. Harnett had paused only to issue instructions that Truthful was to be conveyed incognito to the side door of an office in Whitehall where she would be met and "assisted in returning to her home."

Still white-faced and with an aching head, Truthful soon found herself in Whitehall, beyond that side door, sitting in an armchair in an obscure antechamber without a very clear recollection of how she had got there, Captain Boling having bowed himself out a minute before.

"Ah, Chevalier de Vienne!"

Truthful turned slowly to the inner door, her large hat shadowing her face. General Leye stood there beaming, with an aged servant behind him carrying a silver tray on which rested a tea service and a basket of buttered muffins. The general settled himself in the chair opposite Truthful while the servant arranged the tea and muffins on the table.

"Thank you, Menton. That will be all until I ring."

"Yes, sir. May I remind the general of your appointment with the Duke for breakfast?"

"Yes, yes, I won't be long. Off you go."

General Leye waited until Menton had shut the door, then he reached into a waistcoat pocket and took out a hairy object that it took Truthful a moment to recognize as the false moustache she had been sporting in her male disguise.

"I've taken the liberty of recasting the glamour," said

General Leye. He reached into another pocket and took out a small bottle of gum arabic. "Best put it on again, Lady Truthful. You'll still need to keep that cloak and hat, of course, but best to have belt *and* braces, hey?"

Truthful silently complied, smoothing the moustache on under her nose while the general poured the tea and handed her a cup. He didn't speak until she had taken several sips and had put the cup back down again to reach for a buttered muffin.

"Charles told me about your sea anchor and so forth," he said. "Excellent work. We've been after that Fontaine fellow for some time."

"He told you?" asked Truthful, barely swallowing in time to not be talking through a mouthful of crumbs.

"We had a quick chat," said General Leye. "He was keen to get after Lady Plathenden again. Charles is the very devil for work."

"I see," said Truthful. Harnett was very keen to get away from her, she thought sadly. "What has happened to Lady Plathenden? And the Emerald?"

"I'm afraid we don't rightly know. We had thought she was also on the *Undine*, hidden below, but she wasn't. Now it seems she took a smaller boat upriver. But I have rather a lot of people looking for her now, so I expect we shall find her presently."

"Thank you," said Truthful wearily. None of it seemed to matter very much to her now.

"No, I thank you," said the general. "The more we look into Lady Plathenden the less I like what we've found. She's definitely a malign sorceress, and I fear that her desire for the Emerald has always been about its potential power. There is also some . . ."

He hesitated, as if uncertain whether to continue, then leaned closer and added in a whisper, "There is also a strong suggestion that she has been working with Bonaparte for years, hence her connection with Fontaine. Now one of our smart chaps at the Royal thinks it possible that your Emerald's weather-working magics are in fact only a small part of its true power, and come from its dominion over air and water. But worse than that, he suspects it is one of the legendary stones that grants power over all *four* elements. If it does in fact control fire and, most important, earth magics, it could potentially be used to free Napoleon from the Rock."

"What!" exclaimed Truthful, lowering her voice as Leye made hushing motions with his hands. "But I thought that was impossible! Wasn't that the point of imprisoning him there? I always wondered why he wasn't just . . . just executed like the poor old French king."

"Can't kill him," said Leye shortly. "Hang a master of death magic, that's like giving a thief the key to your front door. But it was thought he'd be safe enough, there being very few talismans of the right kind and the power to release him, and all of them secure. No one considered the Newington Emerald, not till now. But looking into it, that stone is considerably older than was ever thought and certainly a damn sight more powerful than is safe. When we get it back it'll have to go to the treasure room in the Tower of London. You'll be compensated, of course."

"Father will need to at least see it first," said Truthful doubtfully. "I'm sure he'll get better if he can just hold it in his hand. But apart from that I'm sure he'd be happy for the authorities to take charge of it, considering the circumstances."

"Yes, yes," said Leye. "That can all be arranged. Have to find Plathenden first, of course, wrestle it from her. Fortunately she won't have had time to learn how to use its powers."

"Oh," said Truthful. "She could use it? I thought only our family . . ."

"Very tricky things, talismans of that sort," said the general. "Particularly if you haven't the right to them. But a skilled and determined sorceress like Amelia Plathenden would be able to work around that, given time. Time I trust she shall not have. Now, I have a coach waiting to take you back to your great-aunt's, and the sooner the better, so she will stop pestering me about your safety."

"You mean I just . . . just go back to Grosvenor Square and carry on as Lady Truthful?"

"Yes," said General Leye, lifting himself heavily out of his chair. "I mean exactly that. Your stolen Emerald has become a matter of state, and is being treated as such. There's no place for anyone else to be chasing around for it. Too dangerous, apart from anything else."

"I see," said Truthful, lifting her chin mulishly.

"Not that we aren't *extremely* grateful for your assistance," said General Leye. "As I said, none of this would have come to light without you. Well done!"

"Yes," said Truthful. Her head sank back down. She felt very low. Harnett hadn't even bothered to talk to her, to discuss why she had felt it necessary to deceive not only him but the world. Now she was being dismissed from the further pursuit of Lady Plathenden and the Emerald when it was her business. Family business.

But she was too weary to fight about it for the moment. She let General Leye take her arm and escort her out to a waiting carriage and hand her up into its dark interior, the curtains being drawn close. It felt very much like going into exile, she thought, though obviously not as extreme as the one Emperor Napoleon had suffered, being sorcerously forced into the Rock of Gibraltar.

If her Emerald was strong enough to remove a prisoner buried half a mile deep in solid granite, what else could it do?

+ ———————— +

Lady Badgery had clearly been warned to expect her, for even though it was still not yet eight o'clock in the morning, Dworkin was waiting outside the front door. As soon as he saw the coach arrive, he hurried down the front steps.

"Master de Vienne! You are anxiously awaited."

"Thank you, Dworkin," croaked Truthful. She stepped down from the coach and ran up the front steps, keeping her head down, the disreputable broad-brimmed hat shielding her face. Presuming the glamour was holding, this would aid in the impression of a penitent young man returning from some ill-advised expedition. "I am sorry to put everyone out."

"Her ladyship said that you would probably wish to retire immediately," said Dworkin, keeping pace a few steps behind her. "However, if she might have some brief conversation first?"

"Of course," said Truthful. "I will go to her ladyship at once."

Lady Badgery was, for once, not in bed. She was pacing around in her blue saloon, with her fez on her head and a very strange robe made up of many small white furs over her shoulders. As Parkins opened the door to admit Truthful,

Lady Badgery let out a shriek and rushed over to embrace her great-niece.

"My dear! You're safe!"

Parkins edged out and shut the door behind her. Lady Badgery took Truthful's hands and drew her over so they could sit next to each other on an elegant sofa covered in blue silk shot with gold.

"Where did you get that awful hat? And that cloak?"

"Captain Boling of the *Lyonesse* gave them to me," said Truthful, taking both items off with some relief. "I'm afraid your glamour was dissipated by the sea, Great-aunt. General Leye ensorcelled it again for me."

"Hmmm," said Lady Badgery, staring intently at Truthful's upper lip and then away and back again, gauging the efficacy of the glamour. "An elegant sorcerer, Ned. Very fine work. But tell me everything! How did you come to be at *sea*? And what has happened to the handsome Major Harnett?"

Truthful looked down at her hands, clasped in her lap.

"Major Harnett was with me. But he was very discomposed to discover that I was a girl and he didn't know it," she said with a gulp. "And I think embarrassed beyond bearing when he was unable to rescue me, and my small efforts . . . In any case, I doubt I will see him again. He and General Leye don't want my help to find the Emerald anymore. Apparently it has become a matter of state!"

"I see," said Lady Badgery, who did indeed see, far more than Truthful was actually saying. "Why don't you tell me exactly what has occurred. Then you can have a bath and a rest and we can comfortably consider what—if anything—is to be done."

Truthful told her. At least she told her what had happened, not going into any detail about how she felt. Partly because she wasn't sure how she felt, apart from being extremely aggrieved that Harnett hadn't bothered to talk to her, and obviously thought she had done something very wrong in assuming her disguise.

But she did feel somewhat better after describing the events of the previous night and day. Lady Badgery laughed at much of it, and was suitably impressed with Truthful's cleverness in making the sea anchor and in causing the *Undine* to broach to and thus be caught.

"You are a real heroine," she said finally. "Now you must bathe and rest. Put the chevalier to rest too, I think. You must be all Lady Truthful Newington for the ball tonight."

"Ball? What ball?" asked Truthful.

"Why, Lady Mournbeck's of course!" exclaimed Lady Badgery. "Had you forgotten? Madame Lapointe has sent over your new dress, the ivory silk."

"I can't think of balls and gowns now," fretted Truthful.

"Truthful!" exclaimed Lady Badgery. "It is a very important ball. Cecilie Mournbeck, besides being one of my friends, is an acknowledged leader of the *ton*. Everyone will be there, and there will be many people eager to meet or renew their acquaintance with you. Most of them eligible young men, I have to say."

"I don't care about eligible young men," snapped Truthful.

Lady Badgery's imposing eyebrows arched up to become almost triangular.

"But you do care about one possibly ineligible young man?" she asked gently.

"No," said Truthful. "Not at all. None! I must go and take my bath!"

She sprang up and left the room hurriedly. Lady Badgery smiled and once more took up the copy of the *Peerage* she had laid under a cushion, to study the alarmingly short entry on the Harnetts. At least they were in there, she comforted herself. The head of the house was only a baronet, to be sure, and it was curious that his second son, a major, had the Christian name James rather than Charles. . . .

Lady Badgery frowned and rang her bell. Dworkin entered and bowed in his impassive manner, his face showing no emotion as his employer instructed him to make inquiries about a Major Harnett, Charles or possibly James or some combination of the two, of Ruswarp in Yorkshire, formerly of the 95th Rifles. If possible, Lady Badgery wished to ascertain his lodging and anything that could be discovered about his friends, his family, and, most important of all, his wealth.

12

GENTLEMEN VISITORS

By the time Truthful had carefully put away her ensorcelled moustache, soaked in her lemon verbena–scented bath, slept for an hour, and dressed in a charming walking dress of green crape with puffed sleeves embellished with silver knot ribbons, she felt much better. After a light luncheon she felt almost completely normal and certainly more able to contemplate Lady Mournbeck's grand ball.

But Truthful had no sooner begun to practice her waltz steps—though she was well aware she could not actually waltz in public until after her presentation—when Dworkin knocked on the door of the small parlor Lady Badgery had given to Truthful to use as her own. After knocking, he uttered one of his distinctive coughs, a sound somewhat like a discontented badger.

"Enter!"

Dworkin stepped inside and stood at attention, the presence of a calling card on the silver salver he held indicating that he was about to announce a visitor. In his own time, the matter clearly not to be rushed.

"Yes, Dworkin?"

"Two gentlemen callers, milady," intoned Dworkin. He proffered the salver. "Your cousin Stephen Newington-Lacy."

Truthful looked at the card on the salver. What was Stephen doing here? she wondered. She had supposed him to already be on his way to Istanbul or wherever it was he had mentioned. But her thoughts moved rapidly on from Stephen to the possibility of who the other caller might be.

"And the other gentleman?" she asked, her heart speeding up. She felt suddenly breathless, and had to keep her lips firmly fastened to not let out an unladylike gasp.

"The military gentleman who came with the chevalier the other . . . ahem . . . evening," said Dworkin. "No card. Major Harnett."

Truthful bit her lip. She couldn't decide whether she wanted to see Harnett or not. He had been so cold, so ungrateful! But perhaps he had come to apologize . . . or maybe even to enlist her help again. There might be something she could do that he could not. The Emerald was hers, after all, at least until it was recovered and handed over to the Crown to be safely stored away in the Tower of London.

"I will see Mr. Newington-Lacy now," she said. "Please ask Major Harnett to wait."

"Yes, milady," said Dworkin. "I will show Mr. Newington-Lacy into the blue saloon."

Truthful opened her mouth to protest that Stephen could perfectly well visit her in her own parlor, but didn't speak. Dworkin wouldn't listen anyway, she knew. She picked up her silk-embroidered reticule and went after him, knowing full well that by the time she got to the blue saloon there would be a maid tidying the big sewing box, to preserve Dworkin's antique notions of sensibility, and doubtless a footman in the corner with a tray offering morning refreshments as well.

She was only slightly wrong. Instead of a maid, Parkins was sorting the sewing box. She stood and curtsied as Truthful came on, not even attempting to disguise a knowing smile. However, there was no footman.

Stephen was ushered in a few minutes later. He was dressed for riding, in sober attire that would have earned the Admiral's approbation, though the cut of his coat and his highly polished but not absolutely brilliant top boots would mark him as a country gentleman to any knowledgeable observer in the metropolis. His moustache did him no favors either, having signally failed to show the luxurious growth he no doubt desired. It looked rather forlorn, sparser even than the fake moustache Truthful wore when she was being the chevalier.

Truthful ran to him and he took her hands with a smile, giving her fingers a casual kiss in about as loving a fashion as he would greet a favorite hound.

"Stephen, I am so pleased to see you!" exclaimed Truthful. "I had thought you must already be at sea, or on the Continent!"

"Ah," said Stephen. He looked considerably abashed. "That's why I've come to town. Had to talk to you about that."

"Why?" asked Truthful. "What's happened? Is your mother—"

"No, no, Mother's doing very well," said Stephen. He looked across at Parkins, who was intent on sorting threads. "Now, at least. The truth is . . ."

He faltered, lowered his voice, and leaned in close.

"The truth is, we *were* all rather foxed that day, and when we got home Father took us to task for it, and what with one thing and another, it came out what we intended to do. Mother fainted away, and well . . . we had to promise *not* to do what we said we would. I'm very sorry, Truthful. We drew lots as to who should come and tell you."

"Oh, I am glad," said Truthful. "I did wonder if it was terribly sensible of you all, and Robert still to finish at Harrow, but you were so eager . . ."

"Pot valiant," said Stephen. "I'll be wary of Hetherington's punch from now on, I assure you!"

Truthful laughed.

"Have you called upon my father since I left? Dr. Doyle sends me notes, but they are very brief and he will use Latin, so it is difficult for me to tell Father's true condition."

"I have not," said Stephen. "But Mother did visit last Sunday. He is no longer feverish, it seems, but still confined to bed. He did not repeat his accusation against us, but I doubt he would to Mother, in any case."

Truthful lowered her head, momentarily cast down by the thought of her father still ill, and the vile calumny that had gotten abroad about her cousins and the Emerald.

"Don't fret, Truthful," said Stephen. "No one of any consequence believes we had anything to do with the theft of the Emerald."

Truthful drew in a deep breath and nodded. If Stephen

could carry on as if he didn't care about the slander, so could she.

"I am so glad you're here," she said. "Do you make a long stay in London? There is to be a ball tonight at Lady Mournbeck's; to have a friend there would be—"

"No, no!" cried Stephen. "I am not lingering in the metropolis, and certainly not attending any balls. In fact, I must be on my way. Cripley's have found a third edition of *The Red Annals* for me. I'll pick that up and then I have a lecture to attend. I'm dining with Prestwick after that—my old tutor, you know—I'll rack up with him tonight, and home tomorrow."

"Oh, Stephen," sighed Truthful. "It's only one ball."

"One too many," said Stephen. "About the Emerald, Truthful. I've thought on the matter and it occurs to me we might have all been on the wrong track. A storm-sprite couldn't have picked it up. That maid of yours, Agatha—"

"Yes, she stole it," interrupted Truthful. "For her employer, Lady Amelia Plathenden. She was almost certainly placed with me for just such an opportunity, even though it took years."

Stephen whistled.

"Plathenden, hey? I've heard of her. Her husband was executed in '92 or '93, *hostis humani generis*."

"Enemy . . . something," guessed Truthful.

"Enemy of humanity," said Stephen. "About as bad a malignant sorcerer as you can get. A veritable necromancer, by all accounts."

"How do you know these things, Stephen?" asked Truthful.

"I read," replied Stephen, putting a finger to the side of his nose. "Application. A retentive mind. Things strange to you, Newt, though I suppose—"

He was interrupted in mid-speech by the sudden appearance of Major Harnett, who erupted into the room with Dworkin holding on to his elbow in a vain effort to restrain him without appearing to do so.

"Lady Truthful!" barked Harnett. "I haven't got time to be waiting for your chitchat to be finished. We have important matters to discuss."

"Who is this fellow?" asked Stephen. He stepped forward, his hands bunching into fists. "How dare you break in on my cousin like this, sir!"

"Your cousin?" asked Harnett. He looked Stephen up and down with disdain, paying particular attention to his moustache. "Don't tell me this is the original Frenchman!"

"Frenchman?" asked Stephen. "I'm as English as anyone, damn your eyes!"

"Major Harnett! Stephen!" said Truthful angrily. "This is not some alehouse where you can belabor each other.

Have some consideration for my great-aunt, even if you have none for me!"

The two men glowered at each other. Dworkin released Harnett's coat sleeve and stepped back. Parkins looked back down to her threads, surreptitiously slipping the silver scissors she'd taken up back into place in the basket.

"Stephen Newington-Lacy," said Stephen, after a moment, inclining his head in what could be judiciously accepted as a bow.

Harnett hesitated for a moment, then returned it.

"Major Charles Harnett," he said briefly. "Acting under the orders of General Leye. Here on official business."

"Ah," said Stephen. "The Emerald."

"Does everybody know about it?" exploded Harnett. "Lady Truthful, I had hoped that you might display some discretion—"

"Stephen was there when it disappear . . . when it was stolen," interjected Truthful. Her cheeks were white with anger. "If you are indeed here on official business, I suggest you get on with it."

"Ah," said Harnett. "One of those cousins. The ones that offered to help."

"Yes," said Truthful. "Kindly and *politely* offered to help."

Stephen glanced at Truthful and then at Harnett. They

were staring angrily at each other. He might as well not even be in the room.

"Don't mind me," he said. "I was just going anyway. Have to catch Cripley before he shuts up shop."

"I'm sorry, Stephen," said Truthful. She took his hand and squeezed it. "Thank you for coming to see me and explaining about . . . well, explaining. Do give my best to your parents and Edmund and Robert."

"I will," promised Stephen. He bowed again very correctly to Harnett. "Sir."

Harnett had the grace to look embarrassed.

"I apologize for my unseemly behavior, Mr. Newington-Lacy," he said. "The theft of Lady Truthful's Emerald has become a matter of state and it . . . ahem . . . weighs heavily on my mind."

"I am sure it does," said Stephen, with the swiftest of sideways glances to Truthful. "Be careful, Newt."

"Newt?" exclaimed Harnett.

Truthful ignored him.

"Show Mister Newington-Lacy out, please, Dworkin," she said. "Parkins, you may go too."

There was a moment when Truthful thought she might not be obeyed. But Dworkin looked at Parkins, and though no visible signal was passed, he bowed and opened the door for Stephen. Parkins gathered up her skirts and departed in their wake, pausing only to curtsy on the way.

"Now that we are alone you can berate me to your heart's content," said Truthful. "Though I cannot understand why you are so angry! I told you that I only disguised myself because I had no one else who could find the Emerald."

"What about your cousins?" asked Harnett.

"I had thought them gone on their own searches elsewhere," said Truthful stiffly.

Harnett gave a grim chuckle. "Idiotic boys!"

"How dare you speak of my cousins in such a . . . such a beastly way!" said Truthful. "Besides, if I hadn't dressed as a man and been captured with you, then you'd be drowned by now!"

Harnett's fists clenched and he took a step toward Truthful, but before she could do anything but return his angry stare, he bent his head and his fingers uncurled. With a long sigh, he sank down into the chair opposite Truthful and ran his fingers through his luxuriant hair.

"I am aware that you saved my life," he said slowly. "I have not been sufficiently grateful, I know; I am not quick to . . . deal with certain surprises. I also regret that I put your life in danger. Your life and your reputation."

"I made that choice when I assumed the identity of the Chevalier de Vienne," said Truthful. She spoke warily, not sure whether this new composed Harnett was any easier to deal with than the old angry one.

"I do not think you really knew what you were doing," said Harnett. "You don't seem to understand the consequences of your masquerade, Lady Truthful."

"What consequences?" asked Truthful. "And more to the point, what is this 'official business' you want to discuss with me?"

"Business? Oh, there is a concern Lady Plathenden may try to kidnap you, to help her with the Emerald. Such talismans often respond more easily to a familiar bloodline, and she would hope to compel you to assist her in mastering the stone. However, I have sent for men to watch the house and protect you, so there is no cause for alarm."

"I am not alarmed," said Truthful proudly, though in truth, she was quite perturbed. "I presume this means you haven't captured her?"

"Not yet," said Harnett. He clasped his hands together nervously, and stood up again. "But let us return to the matter of your reputation, Lady Truthful. I recognize that having compromised you—"

"What! Compromised me? How?"

"We were tied up in a barrel together," said Harnett slowly. "For some considerable time. We slept . . ."

"I was dressed as a man," said Truthful defiantly.

"That detail will only exacerbate the interest of ill-wishers," said Harnett. He adjusted his neckcloth and cleared his throat. "This being the case, the only course of action . . . the correct thing . . . I must offer . . . that is to say . . . you have to marry me, Lady Truthful."

Truthful stared up at him. He met her gaze, but it was the look of a spaniel being dragged to an unwanted bath.

"You don't want to marry me, do you?" she asked conversationally, though she didn't know how she was able to sound so perfectly calm. Inside she felt a curious mixture of absolute rage and crushing regret.

Harnett did not immediately answer. His mouth moved a little before he eventually spoke. He did not look at Truthful, and his voice was low.

"I . . . I don't think . . . I don't wish to marry anyone. However, I recognize that I have compromised you and therefore *must* marry you. There is also something else I need to tell you that has considerable bearing on the—"

"Get out!" hissed Truthful. "Get out! I wouldn't marry you even if we'd spent *three* days and nights in a barrel together!"

"Truthful, please listen to me! I have to tell you—"

Whatever he wanted to say was cut off by the sound of an explosion. The room instantly dimmed as thick clouds of sulphurous smoke boiled up from the street, obscuring the sunlight outside the windows. Everything was silent for a long second, then there came a sudden hubbub of shouts and cries from outside.

"Malignant sorcery!" snapped Harnett, and leaped for the door with Truthful at his heels.

13

HYSSOP AND RUE

"Brooms, where are the brooms?" Harnett shouted as he charged down the main staircase toward the front door. Dark yellow, evil-smelling smoke was coiling in under the sill and puffing up into the entry hall, long wafts that moved like tendrils motivated by some cold intelligence and not at all like natural smoke.

Harnett was calling for the brooms of hyssop and rue that by law had to be on hand in every household, for their efficacy in dispersing malignant sorcery. Indeed, in the past such brooms had even been used on the *persons* of malignant sorcerers, though in those cases it was often the broom handle brought down on an unprotected pate that had done the trick, rather than the brush end of straw intermingled with cuttings of herb-of-grace and *Hyssopus officinalis*.

Almost as Harnett shouted, Dworkin emerged from his pantry, a hyssop and rue broom in hand. Parkins popped out from the lower saloon, similarly equipped, and Cook emerged from the kitchen with an impressively large broom, the kitchen maids behind her waving long strings of garlic and bunches of rosemary.

None made as grand an entrance as Lady Badgery, who strode out onto the first-floor landing in her fur-lined robe of watered silk, a silver-tipped ivory wand in her hand. She pointed it firmly at the front door and declaimed in a strong, commanding voice:

> *"Brimstone and sulphur I revoke*
> *Begone ye spirits of fog and smoke*
> *This is not your place, not here*
> *Sweet hyssop and rue, sweep all clear."*

A very strong smell of new-cut herbs rolled down the stairs. The sulphurous smoke shrank back from it, coils spinning widdershins as they retreated under the door. Lady Badgery advanced down the stair, her wand held steady, while the servants lashed the air with their brooms, the eddying gusts they created breaking up the remnant clouds. Harnett took up one of the brooms brought in by a footman and joined the cleansing, but Truthful rushed to the bay window on the left of the door and looked out.

The sorcerous yellow fog was still very thick outside, but she could just discern her cousin's familiar bay mare with the white patch over her eye, staggered to her knees on the road. Behind the horse, blurred silhouettes came into view, servants from the neighboring houses beginning to flail about with brooms.

"Stephen!" cried Truthful, and rushed to the door. But even as she turned the handle to open it, Harnett caught her wrist and stopped her.

"Wait!" he commanded. "We do not know the nature of the fog. It will be banished soon. Lady Badgery has quelled its spread, and the brooms will clear it in a few minutes."

"Stephen might not have a few minutes," said Truthful fiercely. But she did not try to break free of Harnett's grasp. Instead, she slowly raised her hands and set her palms against the door, so she might feel the timber, and through it the air outside. Harnett did not let go, but his grip was light, as if they danced together.

Truthful reached out to the air above and around the house. It would have been easier in the open, under the sky, but she still felt the movement of the wind high above. She called to it with all the magic in her being, directing that breeze to come down, to bowl along the street and sweep away the choking fog that lingered where it should not.

The breeze answered. Shutters rattled, windows shook. Leaves swirled up from the gutters, dark spots in the fog. The yellow smoke thinned, divided, and then was gone as if it had never been, and there were people chasing their hats down the street, brooms on their shoulders, as if some strange new game had just been invented.

Harnett let go of Truthful's wrist. She opened the door and ran down the steps. Stephen's mare was struggling to get up, her eyes wild. Instinctively she ran to her and took the bridle, helping the horse to rise, stroking her neck and whispering soothing words. As always with Truthful and horses, the mare quieted almost immediately. But Truthful's actions were all instinct, her conscious mind intent on Stephen. She looked around desperately for him, expecting to see him thrown and injured.

But there was no sign of him. He wasn't anywhere nearby.

As far as she could see he wasn't in the square at all, not on the street and not over the road in the square garden.

"Where is Stephen?" she asked plaintively, looking back at Harnett, who was carefully looking across the square. He had a pocket pistol in his hand, she noted, and the expression of someone who strongly desired a suitable target.

A watchman who looked strangely familiar to Truthful ran over to Harnett.

"They took him, sir," he gasped. "A hackney comes up alongside of him as he mounted, they grappled him across, and then the brimstone cloud—"

"And where were you, Sergeant Ruggins?" demanded Harnett. "And where are Culpepper and Roach?"

"They've gone after the hackney," said the unfortunate Ruggins. "I was only across the way, sir, honest I was, but they was too quick and then the cloud—"

"Very well," snapped Harnett. "I'll speak to you later. Lady Truthful, you had best return inside the house."

"I have to rescue Stephen," protested Truthful. "Where did this hackney go?"

"My men are already following the hackney," said Harnett. "Please, Lady Truthful. You may still be in danger, it would be best to go inside."

"But why would someone take Stephen!" exclaimed Truthful, staring across the square. There were no hackneys in sight, only servants returning to their houses, brooms in hand, and several gardeners in the central square scratching their heads and eyeing a fallen branch torn off by the wind.

"I regret to say the kidnappers were undoubtedly in Lady Plathenden's employ. They would have thought he was you and, as I said, needed to assist with the Emerald," said Harnett quietly.

"How could they think Stephen was me?"

"You in your French persona," said Harnett quietly. "You are much alike in that case, moustaches and all."

"But . . . but . . . how would Lady Plathenden know about me . . . about being the chevalier?" asked Truthful.

Harnett leaned in even closer and whispered.

"Fontaine had pigeons aboard the *Undine*," he said. "Upon questioning, the crew reported they were regularly used to apprise Fontaine's masters or fellows of his activities, and two were known to fly after our removal from the barrel. So we must suppose that Lady Plathenden *does* know you and Henri de Vienne are the same person. That is what I meant by you being compromised more than you think, because if Lady Plathenden knows then others may know too. Now, if you would allow me a few minutes I must tell you—"

He spoke to empty air, because Truthful was stalking up the steps of the house. She tried to slam the front door behind her in Harnett's face, but it was too heavy. He arrested it easily and followed her in.

Lady Badgery was in the hallway, wand still in her hand.

"A fine way to wake up an old lady from her well-deserved afternoon rest," she declared. "Are we all to be slain in our beds?"

"Not this time, Lady Badgery," replied Harnett. "But I fear your great-nephew has been kidnapped, presumably by servants of Lady Plathenden."

"My great-nephew?" asked Lady Badgery, her eyebrows rising. The only great-nephew she possessed was a babe of three, and presumed safe with his parents in Gloucestershire. "But how—"

"No, not Great-aunt's great-nephew," interrupted Truthful quickly. "Stephen Newington-*Lacy*. The other side of the family."

"This sort of thing never happened when I was a girl," grumbled Lady Badgery.

"No, I believe it was much worse," said Truthful, taking her great-aunt's arm. "Shall I escort you back to your bedchamber?"

"Not yet!" snapped Lady Badgery. "I want to know what is happening, and in any case, we have a guest!"

"I believe Major Harnett is just leaving," said Truthful. The words had barely left her mouth before she regretted them, and not only because she would need Harnett's help to rescue Stephen.

"No, I am not," said Harnett decisively. "Lady Badgery, your skill as a diviner is well known. Could I prevail upon you to seek out Stephen Newington-Lacy's whereabouts? I think it is very likely he is being taken to wherever Lady

Plathenden is hiding. If you could scry him on his way before he comes under the aegis of the Emerald—"

Lady Badgery shook her head.

"I fear not," she said. "That dismal cloud was very strong and pressed hard upon the house. It took all my strength to turn it back outside. I dare not attempt a divination or other sorcery until I have rested. But surely you have diviners in government service?"

"It would take too long to fetch one here, where the signatures are fresh," said Harnett. "It seems I must rely on my men keeping the hackney in sight. . . ."

He did not sound very confident.

"And I must go and change my dress," said Truthful. Without thinking, she touched her upper lip where her moustache would be affixed. Once more disguised as the chevalier, she could go forth in search of Stephen.

"Change your dress?" asked Lady Badgery. She clearly knew what Truthful was intending, and drew the young woman closer to her with a bony, heavily ringed hand. "No, dear. I am going to lie down and you will read to me until it is time to prepare for Lady Mournbeck's ball."

"Great-aunt!" protested Truthful. "We can't go to the ball with Stephen kidnapped!"

"Yes, we can," said Lady Badgery. "In fact we must. It is of the first importance that we appear to be unruffled by any such happening. If you are asked of it, which I doubt, you will smile and say 'boys will be boys' or words to that effect. We must take care that your reputation is not any more . . . that is, we must be careful."

"If I might beg a few words with you first, Lady Truthful," said Harnett. "There really is something very important that I need to tell you—"

"Now, now, Major Harnett," said Lady Badgery. "We have all had quite a shock, and I must lie down. By the way, is your first name Charles or James?"

"Charles," said Harnett automatically. He frowned and turned his attention away from Truthful to Lady Badgery. "That is, I can explain, Lady Badgery. If you would allow me—"

"Oh, why aren't you out searching for Stephen!" cried out Truthful. "If I was a man I wouldn't be prosing on forever here when someone is in so much danger!"

"I am sure my men will find him," retorted Harnett. "And the Emerald! And I do not need to be told my duty, or rather my several duties, which I am attempting to do if only you would let me get a word in edgeways!"

"You are unbearable!" gasped Truthful. Wrenching herself from her great-aunt's grip, she ran up the stairs.

Harnett took a deep breath and turned once more to Lady Badgery, who inclined her head and gave him an encouraging smile.

"Lady Badgery, the truth is that acting under information received and in the haste of the moment, I was forced to assume—"

"Sir! Sir! Roach is here! Them kidnappers overturned their hack on Seymour Street!"

Ruggins was calling excitedly through the open doorway. Out on the street behind him, a plainly dressed man on horseback with the tough look of former military service and a small golden crown in the buttonhole of his blue coat waved to Harnett.

"We got one of 'em, sir! Culpepper and some locals 'ave took him to the roundhouse!"

"And the kidnapped young man?" asked Harnett quickly.

"Him too, he's a right game one, he did summat sorcerouslike to the horses," said Roach. "Made 'em bolt on the corner, so they clipped the gutter and went all arsy-versy."

"I must go," snapped Harnett to Lady Badgery. "Your servant, ma'am!"

He was down the steps in only two paces, but at the street he paused and called back.

"Keep Lady Truthful safe! I will dispatch men to guard the house!"

14

A GIFT AND A LETTER

It took the news that Stephen was rescued, in addition to all of Lady Badgery's persuasive powers and the authority of being in loco parentis to make sure Truthful did not immediately don her disguise and issue forth to Seymour Street to see exactly what was happening. Fortunately she did not have to wait very long before one of Harnett's men arrived bearing a message from the Major that both relieved and infuriated Truthful.

"Stephen appears to be entirely unscathed," she said to Lady Badgery, who was lying on her bed, well supported by a vast pile of silken pillows. "Harnett says he is in high grig and is now assisting in the search for the would-be abductor that escaped in the hope he will lead them to Lady Plathenden and the Emerald!"

"I am relieved he is unhurt," said Lady Badgery. "And of course he would want to take part in bringing the criminals to justice."

"While I must wait here," complained Truthful. "And go to a tiresome ball tonight, even though it is *my* Emerald!"

"You did not think the prospect of so grand a ball as Lady Mournbeck's tiresome a scant few days ago," said Lady Badgery. "I recollect you said to me you had never in your life attended so grand an affair and you were most excited!"

"Well, I own that I was then," said Truthful. She frowned. "But I hadn't seen Lady Plathenden with *my* Emerald, or been tied up in a barrel with . . . It all makes such things as balls seem less . . . less consequential."

"They can be of great consequence," said Lady Badgery. "It was at just such a ball that your father first set eyes upon your mother, and indeed, I first clasped hands with my poor departed Badgery. You might well chance upon your own future husband at the ball this evening, Truthful."

"I very much doubt that," said Truthful, blushing and avoiding her great-aunt's rather too searching gaze. "I think . . . I think I may never marry. I shall look after Father and remain in the country."

"Humph," said Lady Badgery. Truthful was unsure what this sound actually meant, though it did seem the old lady was either expressing doubt or amusement at Truthful's rather high-blown pronouncement. Or perhaps something of both. "You can read to me now, and then I shall sleep until supper."

As Parkins helped her dress that evening, Truthful *did* recapture a little of her previous excitement about the prospect of going to her first grand London ball. The ivory silk gown with its delicate gold tracery was the most beautiful dress she had ever worn, and was perfectly complemented by a Norwich shawl of the highest quality; new and vastly elegant elbow-length gloves; and a fan of peacock-pattern silk between ivory sticks. As became a young lady who had not yet been presented but was in the process of coming out, her only jewelry was a very plain necklace of slim gold beads, and her hair was dressed with an elegant simplicity, Truthful being amazed at how Parkins could make it so fashionable despite the cut that had made it possible for her to look the gentleman.

When Parkins adjudged her completely ready Truthful went down to join Lady Badgery, who was opening a missive that had just been delivered. The dowager, resplendent in a dress of yesteryear that combined panels of purple and green silk over a voluminous petticoat possibly supported by some sort of underwiring, brandished the letter at Truthful triumphantly, almost upsetting the enormous feathered turban that was pinned to her head.

"Cecilie has come through," she said.

"Cecilie?" asked Truthful.

"Lady Mournbeck," said her great-aunt. "I had asked her to send a card for her ball to your Major Harnett, and though she initially declined, it seems that upon investigation she is familiar with the major's aunt, Mrs. Gough, who was a Tavilland before her marriage and so is a cousin of some sort to Mournbeck himself. So she has done as I asked, and he will be there."

"He is not *my* Major Harnett," said Truthful mulishly. "And I do not know why you should wish to have him invited. Besides, surely he is too busy finding the Emerald, or at least he should be."

"I like the young man," said Lady Badgery roguishly. "I want to see how he behaves among company."

Truthful did not answer, her feelings about the ball once more confused. She had managed to regain some of her previous simple excitement, the feeling of looking forward to an unalloyed pleasure. Now it was complicated again, not least because she was not sure how she felt. She both wanted to see Harnett again and to never see him again. For the moment, the "never seeing again" feeling was stronger.

She grimaced, holding back a tear as she remembered his admission that he didn't want to marry anyone and his most reluctant offer of marriage to her that he only made due to social convention. He didn't care for her, so she must make sure she did not entertain any feelings for *him*.

These lowering thoughts were interrupted by Dworkin's cough. The butler approached Truthful with a small package wrapped in bright paper and a blue ribbon on his silver tray.

"A present for Lady Truthful," he announced.

"For me?" asked Truthful, surprised. She reached out for it, only to be surprised as the dowager countess suddenly grabbed her elbow.

"Who is it from, Dworkin?" asked Lady Badgery. "Have our temporary guardians seen it?"

"It was brought by Sergeant Ruggins," said Dworkin calmly. "It is from Major Harnett and I believe is of some importance in the protection of Lady Truthful."

"I don't want it," snapped Truthful.

"Don't be silly, my dear," said Lady Badgery. "At least see what it is before you refuse it. It may be in the nature of an official present rather than a personal one, and judging from what happened to your cousin Stephen, we had best be prepared for the worst."

"Very well," sighed Truthful. She took the package and unwrapped it, revealing a folded note and a very old box covered in faded pearly shagreen. Truthful set the box aside on the arm of her chair and read the note.

Dear Lady Truthful,

I regret that due to the continuing investigation into the whereabouts of Lady Plathenden and the Newington Emerald I am unable to call upon you in person, as I would wish, in order to impart to you an important matter and further a discussion I believe to be of paramount importance. I must also warn you that we have not yet ascertained the full extent of Lady Plathenden's scheming, beyond the fact that she has a considerable criminal force in her employ. It is believed that she may still attempt to take your person captive by force or trickery in order to wrest control of the Emerald, so I have taken the liberty of increasing the guard under Sergeant Ruggins. In addition, I am sending you a charmed bracelet that I request you wear for your own protection until such time as Lady Plathenden is arrested and the Emerald is recovered. Please excuse my penmanship, written in haste upon the road.

Yours etc.

"He couldn't even be bothered to sign it," said Truthful. She handed the note to Lady Badgery and picked up the box. Her fingers tingled as she lifted the hook and opened it to reveal a slim and remarkably plain bracelet made of many gold and silver wires twisted together. Truthful slid it over her wrist. It felt a little loose at first, but when she turned it around, she saw that it would not easily come off. Lady Badgery lowered the note and said, "Show me, Truthful!"

Truthful held out her arm. Lady Badgery took her wrist and rotated it so she could examine the bracelet from every angle, being careful not to touch it herself. After several minutes, she gently lowered Truthful's arm and sat back.

"That is an ancient and very powerful charm," she pronounced. "A spell-breaker of the first order. You must be careful not to touch others with it, lest it dissolve any sorcery upon their person. I wonder if your Major Harnett . . . or Ned Leye borrowed it from the museum. It certainly belongs there, if not the Tower."

"I suppose I had better wear it, but I trust it will not be needed," said Truthful. She sighed and added, "I hope that Lady Plathenden is soon arrested and I can go home!"

"I was not aware you disliked staying with an old lady so much," sniffed Lady Badgery.

"Oh no!" exclaimed Truthful. She clasped her great-aunt's hand. "It is just that . . . life at home is . . . easier, I suppose. And I want to show Father the Emerald and make him better."

"We all wish your father better," said Lady Badgery. "However, may I point out that an easier life is not necessarily to be preferred? In any case, it is almost ten o'clock and so we must go. Put your worries behind you now, Truthful, and attempt to enjoy Lady Mournbeck's ball. Or at least successfully pretend to do so."

"I will try, Great-aunt," said Truthful. She forced a smile, maintaining it for several seconds before it slipped away.

"Grimacing won't help," said Lady Badgery as she stood up and shook out her voluminous skirts of gold sateen.

"That was my smile," said Truthful indignantly.

"Was it?" asked Lady Badgery. "Perhaps avoid another one if that is the case. Perhaps you should try to merely look amused. Parkins! Parkins!"

Parkins popped her head around the door and looked inquiringly at her mistress.

"Parkins! My sword cane."

Parkins disappeared again. Truthful looked at her great-aunt.

"A sword cane? Surely that can't be something you can take—"

"It is simply a walking stick for an old and tired woman," said Lady Badgery, "that happens to have a sword in it. But no one will ever know unless it proves necessary to unsheathe it, in which case, it will not matter."

"I see," said Truthful.

"I have a wand in my sleeve as well," said Lady Badgery brightly. "One cannot depend upon Sergeant Ruggins and his type to keep you safe, Truthful. They mean well, but they are only men."

"Yes," said Truthful doubtfully. "Perhaps I should fetch a pistol for myself?"

"Don't be silly!" barked Lady Badgery. "A ball is no place for a pistol. Besides, where would you put it? Let us get on. Dworkin! Dworkin! Has the carriage been brought around?"

The carriage had been brought around to the front. It was very large and rather old-fashioned, and seemed even more so with four liveried footmen hanging off the back, three of them Sergeant Ruggins's men and the fourth Lady Badgery's rather put-out regular servant. Ruggins himself had assumed the role of the driver, and two more of his men stood by with lit flambeaux, to act the part of running footmen who would illuminate the way to Cavendish Square and Lord and Lady Mournbeck's extremely large, palatial, and ugly house.

Truthful and Lady Badgery were handed into the carriage by Dworkin, with what seemed like most of the indoor servants lurking about in the front part of the house, all pretending to carry out tasks with heavy implements that could be turned into makeshift weapons, so they could come to Truthful's rescue should there be another attempt to kidnap her.

There was no such attempt, nor did one seem likely given the number of guards around and on the carriage. Truthful, who had in truth been a little apprehensive, soon forgot she was in any danger and pulled the curtains aside so she could see the outside world.

The significance of Lady Mournbeck's ball could be seen within half a mile of Cavendish Square. Lady Badgery's carriage soon joined a long procession of coaches and sedan chairs waiting their turn to disgorge their passengers on the threshold of 16 Cavendish Square, who would no doubt pause to admire the twin rows, each of a dozen trees, that Lady Mournbeck had arranged along the front of the house in azure tubs. The trees had trunks and branches of silver and leaves of gold, and appeared to be of shining metal but were in fact only cunningly painted, much to the chagrin of the few urchins who had managed to snatch some leaves despite the vast number of watchmen deployed to manage the traffic and quell any possible disturbance that might disrupt the ball.

Given the great press of guests, Lady Badgery and Truthful were not greeted by Lord and Lady Mournbeck until almost eleven o'clock. This all went as expected, Truthful grateful that Lady Mournbeck did not single her out or pause in her greeting of guests to say something embarrassing about inviting Major Harnett.

But Truthful's relief was short-lived. As they entered the vast but already very crowded ballroom Lady Badgery disengaged herself from Truthful's arm.

"I am to see some old friends in the library," she said. "We may play whist. You go and entertain yourself with the young folk, Truthful. Dance if you like, but not the waltz. Not yet."

"Yes, Great-aunt," said Truthful dutifully, but her heart sank as she looked out at the throng. A country dance was nearing its conclusion, with what seemed liked hundreds of participants dancing to the music of the large and accomplished orchestra; every gilded chair against the walls seemed to be occupied, and every circle of beautifully dressed ladies and exquisitely turned-out gentlemen looked to her to be turned inward with the express purpose of keeping her from easily joining them.

But she stood for barely a moment before there was a sudden movement among those circles. Young men turned to look at her, neatly framed just past the doorway, the light from the candles in the great chandelier above making her hair bright as a flame and her green eyes sparkle as if they were indeed emeralds.

In what seemed like only a second later, Truthful found

herself surrounded by gentlemen asking her to make up a set with them for the next quadrille; offering to fetch her a glass of lemonade or champagne or orgeat; wondering if she might like to sit down, or stand up for a country dance; and surely a waltz could be permitted with her presentation only a few weeks away?

None of the gentlemen were Major Harnett. Truthful accepted several invitations to dance from those she had met before, and took particular care to be pleasant to Mr. Trellingsworth, who went away happily once his name was inscribed upon her dance card for the fourth quadrille. But she declined the offer of drinks and chairs, and chose instead to make her way toward that corner of the ballroom which was primarily occupied by other young ladies taking their respite between dances and being modestly seen not to seek the company of the men.

Truthful was almost there when she was intercepted by a dark-haired, serious-looking young woman of no great beauty but some obvious, indefinable charm and a very businesslike manner. This young lady stood in front of her, forcing Truthful to stop, leaned in close, and spoke quietly but forcefully.

"Lady Truthful? I am Miss Gough, Miss Eliza Gough. I should like to speak to you privately on a matter that concerns my fiancé."

"Your fiancé?" asked Truthful, bewildered. She had never met Miss Gough, though her name did sound familiar.

"Yes," said Miss Gough decidedly. "My fiancé, Major Harnett."

15

LADY MOURNBECK'S BALL

"**I** see," said Truthful lightly, though she felt as if she had suddenly been struck somewhere just below her heart with a savage blow. It was only surprise, she told herself as she took a calming breath and tried not to show any agitation. It was very difficult to believe that Harnett had not only made her an offer when he claimed to not want to marry anyone, but he was also already betrothed! Yet here was this serious young lady telling her so . . . but it was of no consequence, Truthful told herself firmly. She only felt upset because she had not thought Harnett so contemptible. That was all.

"We can talk outside on the garden terrace," said Miss Gough, taking Truthful's arm and leading her away. Truthful went with her, her mind in a turmoil.

No one else was on the terrace, though the evening was pleasant, and Lady Mournbeck had been thoughtful enough to have several Japanese lanterns hung to create a charming nook where guests might recoup from the hurly-burly of the ballroom. Miss Gough steered Truthful to a bench, and they both sat down. Truthful flicked her fan open and began to fan her face, but shut it again when she realized she was revealing something of her inner agitation.

"This is difficult," said Miss Gough, indicating that it was not only Truthful who suffered some agitation. "Where to begin?"

She took a very deep breath, held her hands together, and looked Truthful squarely in the eye.

"I want to ask you to . . . to discourage Major Harnett," she said, with a gulp. "And most particularly discourage his mother. I mean discourage any pretension that you might look upon his suit with favor."

"I don't understand," said Truthful. "You say Major Harnett is your fiancé?"

"We have had an informal understanding for some two years," said Miss Gough. "But my mother does not wish me to marry Major Harnett, who is my cousin, and my aunt

Sylvia—that is his mother—she is most desirous that he should marry an heiress. That is why I am asking you to let him go. You are rich, and a beauty, surely you could choose anyone and . . . and I will die if he marries you!"

Truthful reached out and took Miss Gough's trembling hands in her own.

"I have no interest in marrying Major Harnett," she said firmly. "You need not be concerned about me."

"But you asked Lady Mournbeck to invite him tonight," said Miss Gough. "Mother and Aunt Sylvia were cock-a-hoop about it."

Truthful shook her head. "That was none of my doing. It was my great-aunt. I'm not perfectly sure why. She can be a little . . . eccentric at times."

"I couldn't believe you wanted him invited so particularly," said Miss Gough. She took a handkerchief from her sleeve and dabbed her eyes with it. "Or even how he might have come to your notice! But Aunt Sylvia insisted it was so. It is so very difficult when she is against us, and my own mother too, and the book is taking so long . . . we can't get married until it is published and a great success, which I'm sure it will be. Then Aunt Sylvia said you were setting your cap at him . . . and you are so beautiful, and everyone knows rich enough to buy an abbey . . ."

"If Major Harnett truly loves you and you love him then

you have nothing to fear from anyone," said Truthful diplomatically as Miss Gough had a quiet little sob into her handkerchief. "Hadn't we better go back inside? I think I have missed a dance I promised and am in some danger of being forsworn on the next as well."

"Thank you," said Miss Gough, tucking her handkerchief away. Her eyes were a little red, but with some effort she composed her face. "You . . . you won't dance with him tonight, will you? Only it would so encourage his mother if you do."

"I won't," promised Truthful. "I haven't seen Major Harnett at all, I must say, though I suppose that it is no surprise in such a crush."

"Oh, he is always late," said Miss Gough. "In fact, he might not even remember. Sometimes he gets so intent upon his manuscript that he works all night. Why, just this week he rewrote two whole chapters when they were already perfectly good, in my opinion. But I am sure he will soon finish, and the publishers are waiting. They are so eager they have forgone half their usual fee, which is a wonder!"

"I am glad," said Truthful, though she found it hard to reconcile her image of Major Harnett with someone who would work away at his desk all night. Yet another indication that she didn't really know him at all, and would be best off forgetting what she did know. "I am surprised he could find any time to write, what with searching for Lady Plathenden and the Emerald."

Miss Gough gave her a puzzled look, but before she could say anything more, a young man with flaxen hair and a pleasant but vacant face looked out onto the terrace. Seeing Truthful, he smiled and waved. His smile added charm to his visage, but did not alter his essential likeness to an enthusiastic but not overbright puppy.

"Lady Truthful! Our set is being made up! I have been looking for you everywhere."

"And here I am, Sir Evelyn," said Truthful, taking his arm. "I trust we will not be too late?"

"I would be happy to wait for *you* until the end of time," said Sir Evelyn. "Beyond the end of time if it comes to that! Beyond the end of the end of . . . er . . . the end of time, no, that's too many ends—"

"Good-bye, Miss Gough," said Truthful, mercifully cutting Sir Evelyn short before he became more confused.

"Good-bye, Lady Truthful," said Miss Gough. "And thank you."

Truthful smiled, a smile that she feared was indeed a grimace. She hardly heard Sir Evelyn prattling on as they went back inside. The music washed over her as she mechanically took up her place for the quadrille, bowing and smiling, her mind a million miles away and her heart a cold void in her chest as the rest of her trod out the dance as if she cared for nothing else in the world.

Truthful danced every dance save the waltzes after that quadrille, turned down three times as many invitations, and accepted several glasses of lemonade and one of champagne. The fortune hunters she had already met in the Park or at Lady Badgery's house when she first came to town offered her eloquent encomiums, and other, newly acquainted gentlemen delivered less-eloquent but possibly more deeply felt praise. She spoke to several other young ladies, who appeared to fall into two camps: those who admired her beauty and wished to be friends on the strength of it, and those who resented her and considered her a rival in the Marriage Mart.

None of it was of any significance to Truthful. She felt as if she was a play-actor, and not a very good one at that, speaking her lines and treading the boards to her appointed place at the appointed time, but with no feeling. The only real emotion she felt was toward one o'clock in the morning, when Lady Badgery emerged from the library and bore down upon her as she was escorted from the latest country dance by her current swain.

"Ah, Truthful," said Lady Badgery. She tapped Truthful's

partner painfully on the elbow with the knob of her walking stick and added, "Sir Arthur Tennant, I believe. Ain't you the one they call 'Dingle' on account of being lost in Ireland that time?"

An embarrassed mumble, a fumbled bow, and a fast retreat indicated that, as per usual, Lady Badgery was correct.

"Enjoying the ball?" asked Lady Badgery. "You are a veritable hit, Truthful. Got all the mamas talking, and the men . . . well, look at them!"

She waved her stick around dangerously, making several young gentlemen step back and several who had clearly been hoping to engage Truthful's attention suddenly sheer away.

"Yes, Great-aunt," said Truthful dutifully. "But I am tired now and if it would not displease you, would like to go home."

"What?" asked Lady Badgery shrewdly. She peered at Truthful, then looked fiercely around. "Something's upset you, puss, that I can see. One of these fellows overstepped the line?"

"No, nothing like that," said Truthful. "I just have the headache a little. I suppose I am not used to such a crush."

"That fellow Harnett's not here," said Lady Badgery. "Is he?"

"I haven't seen him," said Truthful, avoiding her great-aunt's gaze. "But . . . but I did meet Miss Gough, his . . . his betrothed."

"Ah, that was . . . unfortunate," said Lady Badgery, with a curious sideways glance at Truthful. "Well if you have the headache I suppose we must go home. Certainly I have had no luck at cards, and the champagne is not of the best. Mournbeck always does try to scrimp and Cecilie doesn't touch the stuff, so he gets away with it. Come then. Out of my way, spider-shanks! Fellow with calves like that shouldn't be seen in knee breeches."

Truthful followed her great-aunt, pretending she couldn't hear the imprecations Lady Badgery bestowed on anyone foolish enough to get in her way as she sailed through the crowd. At least until the unstoppable force met an immovable object, in this case an elderly peer and his wife who, rather than moving aside, smiled and spoke in unison, almost as if they had practiced doing so.

"Ermintrude!"

Truthful, half a pace behind her great-aunt, recognized the man immediately. It was Lord Otterbrook, the Marquis of Poole, who had run her post chaise into a ditch.

"Otterbrook, Lucy," replied Lady Badgery. "How nice to see you. Allow me to present my great-niece, Venetia's daughter. Lady Truthful, the Marquis and Marchioness of Poole, Lord and Lady Otterbrook."

"But we've met!" exclaimed the Marquis, raising his quizzing glass to look at Truthful. "I ran your post chaise into a ditch near Maidstone some weeks ago, didn't I?"

"Ah, yes, my lord," said Truthful doubtfully, glancing at the Marchioness, a woman who looked as formidable as her own great-aunt, though she was considerably plumper and not so eccentric in her dress save for the number of rings she wore, including one set with a very large ruby on her left hand, and another with an enormous sapphire on her right. She was staring at Truthful's bracelet, but looked up at Truthful's face as she spoke.

"You do take after dear Venetia," said the Marchioness, taking Truthful's hands and holding them so she might look straight at her face. "I am delighted to make your acquaintance, my dear. Athelstan, we must invite Lady Truthful to our Masquerade Ball!"

"Already have," said the Marquis. "At least, sent Ermintrude a card last week, Lady Truthful naturally presumed to be included."

"I saw it," sniffed Lady Badgery. "But why you should presume to hold a masquerade in Brighton *before* the end of the Season . . . I doubt not it will be a sparse, ill-attended affair."

"That's where you're wrong, Ermintrude," said the Marchioness. "Athelstan has already seen it in the fire, a vast throng and such elegant costumes! It will be the envy of everyone!"

"Athelstan saw it!" exclaimed Lady Badgery. "A third-rate divination is no surety."

"Prinny's coming," said the Marquis, ignoring this slight on his sorcerous powers. "He's going down to look at the progress Nash is making on the pavilion, I told him he might as well make a night of it. Suggested he come as Canute, have some footmen costumed as waves so he can send them back and forth. Bit of fun, hey?"

"I would like to see Brighton," said Truthful, thinking that anywhere would be better than London at the moment, where she might encounter Harnett at any time. She felt defeated and lost. The search for the Emerald had gone into other hands—more capable hands, she told herself—and she felt no joy in London society. Perhaps Brighton and a masquerade ball would distract her. Not to mention a sight of the Prince Regent. It would be interesting to see one of the royal Princes her father detested so much.

"Where would we stay?" asked Lady Badgery. "My house there won't be ready for a month, and there's nowhere else fit for habitation in the damned place. Damp sheets and cold chops!"

"Stay with us," said the Marchioness. "I sent Yardley down last week to furbish everything up. Plenty of room. No other guests."

"Unless my nevvy graces us with his presence," said the Marquis. "Unlikely, but possible. Busy fellow, you know."

"I should like to go, Great-aunt," said Truthful. "I think . . . I think some sea air might do me good."

But even as she spoke, she was thinking of other sea air. Of being in the barrel, close to Harnett, and the breeze through the cracks, heavy with salt . . . she blinked and resolutely tried to put those memories out of her mind.

"Very well," said Lady Badgery, with an alacrity that surprised Truthful. "When are we to come to you, Lucy?"

"The Masquerade is Thursday, at the Old Ship," said the Marchioness. "Wednesday?"

"Thank you for the kind invitation, my lord," said Truthful, remembering her manners. But she also remembered something else. "Oh, I had forgotten!" she said. "We are currently encumbered with law officers, or not precisely . . . but government people, set to protect me from . . . it is an unusual circumstance, but we might need to bring many more servants—"

"Pish!" said the Marquis. "I know all about that!"

Truthful stared at him. Lady Badgery coughed, and the Marchioness sighed.

"That is to say, in the government now, you know!" said Lord Otterbrook. "On a committee with Ned Leye, matter came up. Not poking my nose into your affairs, Lady Truthful!"

"Oh, I see," said Truthful. "But if we do still have them with us, would it not be a frightful crowd for your servants?"

"No, no, there really is plenty of room, we do not have a large staff there," said the Marchioness.

"My predecessor, distant cousin, you know, bought the place. He used to go to Brighthelmstone, as it was, to take the seawater cure," explained the Marquis. "Not that it did him any good. Terrible fellow, but a good eye for a house. Or two, in this case, on the Marine Parade. He had 'em joined together, you know. So you need not fear we'll all be elbow-jostling each other at breakfast. We look forward to you joining us, Lady Badgery, Lady Truthful."

He bowed, Lady Otterbrook took his arm, and they continued on deeper into the ballroom as Truthful curtsied and Lady Badgery gave a kind of nod of farewell.

They continued on their way in the opposite direction, toward the entrance hall, but just before passing through the jam of people in the double doorway, Truthful stumbled and, in regaining her balance, thrust out her arm.

By unlucky chance, her bracelet touched the bare skin

above the elbow of a lady, between her glove and the spider-gauze sleeve of her dress. There was a flash of harsh blue light, followed a moment later by a scream. The lady in question, a moment before a vision of youth and beauty, now appeared at least fifteen years older. Her skin had lost its glow, and her clear blue eyes were clouded and lit not with innocence but fierce anger. Even her dress had lost the sheen of new silk and the diamonds at her neck had grown dull and so likely to be paste.

Fortunately she did not know who had dispelled her glamour, and Lady Badgery hustled Truthful away even as her great-niece opened her mouth to apologize. Behind them they heard the stir of voices, many of them raised in amusement rather than concern, and another angry scream and a shouted denial.

"Oh no," said Truthful, glancing back. "She has slapped some poor innocent! It is my fault! I must go back and explain."

"No you must not," said Lady Badgery. "That was Lady Linniston, and she has got no more than she deserves, the cat! How she has led poor Linniston a dance, with her cicisbei and fancy men. Now all the world can see her as she really is."

"But the woman she slapped—"

"Cordelia Bassingthwaite can more than hold her own," said Lady Badgery. They were in the entrance hall now, and an alert Mournbeck footman had already raced outside. They heard him shouting as other servants brought them their cloaks.

"Lady Badgery's carriage! Lady Badgery's carriage!"

16

PREPARATIONS FOR A MASQUERADE

The short return journey to Grosvenor Square was untroubled by any attempted kidnappings, allowing Truthful to gratefully go to her bed just before two in the morning. But even though she was very tired, sleep evaded her for some considerable time. It was distinctly more difficult in the deep dark of the night to put Harnett out of her mind than it was in the bright daylight, or even when dancing at the ball. But she knew she must. He was clearly not to be trusted, perhaps addicted to the shadowy world of espionage and half-truths or even outright dissimulation.

In any case, he disliked her and was probably still angry

she had deceived him with her masquerade.

And he was going to be married.

Truthful tried to tell herself that she didn't care, that it was impossible to care for someone she had met so recently. She hardly knew him, after all, and most of what she did know of him was how he had behaved when he thought she was a man.

Sleep came to her eventually, but not before tears came that she was ashamed to shed but somehow couldn't stop.

The next morning, barely seen by Truthful as she rose at half past eleven, was bright and cheerful. Sun shone through all the windows, the sky was blue, and the faint sounds of a street sweeper singing "Enchantress, Farewell" came from the corner of the square and South Audley Street.

Truthful looked out with a jaundiced eye. She saw Sergeant Ruggins across the road by the garden railing, pacing backward and forward, glancing every now and then at the house and occasionally back into the garden square. There were a few children and their nannies in the garden, and a cluster of gardeners doing something to a flower bed that required them to gather around and lean on their shovels and forks. Several gentlemen on horseback were riding through on the northern side of the square, a chaise was letting several ladies alight on the eastern side by Number Four . . . all was serene.

Truthful went downstairs and found her great-aunt finishing off a hearty breakfast while looking at a number of charcoal illustrations, character sketches of outlandish style, the uppermost some kind of pirate. The author of these sketches—a large bearded man wearing a strange kind of smock and a knitted cap of violently purple wool—sat at the other end of the table in front of an open drawing box and several blank sheets of paper.

"Ah, Lady Truthful," said her great-aunt. "This is Signor Fraticelli, who makes all my masquerade costumes. He is a genius. He will make yours also."

"What is it that you wish to be at the Masquerade, Lady Truthful?" asked Signor Fraticelli. "A swan perhaps? A Valkyrie? A Wood Fay?"

Truthful blinked sleepily.

"I do not know, signor," she said helplessly. "Perhaps after breakfast . . ."

"I am to be a pirate," said Lady Badgery with satisfaction. "In scarlet, with a belt of linked gold moidores, purple breeches, and a cutlass. I already have several actual cutlasses, of course, from Badgery's grandfather. Get yourself something to eat, Truthful, and think about a costume. Signor Fraticelli is a busy man and we only have four days before we must leave for Brighton. A first-rate costume will take all that time to make."

"Longer," said Signor Fraticelli. "But for Lady Badgery . . . we do the impossible."

"Oh," said Truthful. "I think I shall just have a boiled egg."

"Mary, tell Cook three boiled eggs for Lady Truthful," said Lady Badgery to the maid who was busying herself with a spirit burner under a dish of bacon. "You must keep up your strength, Truthful. I do not want you pining away."

"I am not pining," said Truthful indignantly. "Why should I pine?"

"That's better," replied Lady Badgery. "How about a mermaid?"

"Not a mermaid." Truthful shuddered. "Too awkward, with a long tail. I should like something I can move in!"

"Perhaps Lady Truthful would also like to wear the breeches and dress as a man," said the signor helpfully.

"No!" exclaimed Truthful and Lady Badgery together, though for different reasons.

"No," agreed Signor Fraticelli. "Milady is very beautiful . . . perhaps a goddess? Venus? With a dress of scallops, not painted but fashioned of jade I think . . . no, there is not time."

"Not Venus," said Truthful, after a moment's thought. "Diana. The Huntress. With a real bow. One I can shoot people with if necessary."

"Ah, Diana!" cried the signor, suddenly in raptures. He bent over his paper and began to sketch furiously. "A short under-dress of the whitest silk, over it a tunic of white lace, folded at the neck just so, and high strapped sandals of silver. A simple headdress with a crescent moon set upon it, the scabbard white leather, the buckles silver, but the arrows fletched in deep azure, the only touch of color . . ."

He held up his sketch. Truthful was taken aback to see not a thing of rough charcoal lines but a brilliant image in full color that somehow leaped out of the page—and it was recognizably herself, attired just as Signor Fraticelli had described. Clearly the man was a very talented illusion-maker.

Lady Badgery applauded as the sketch slowly faded back to a charcoal drawing.

"How much?" she asked. "Pirate and Diana, ready by Tuesday evening."

"Four hundred guineas," said Signor Fraticelli without a moment's hesitation.

"Done," said Lady Badgery. "Thank you, signor. You may go."

"At once, Lady Badgery," declared Signor Fraticelli, with a deep bow that almost brought his forehead into violent conflict with the edge of the table. "I must immediately begin my creation!"

He collected his sketches and his box of drawing implements, threw a violently yellow cloak over his shoulders, and stalked from the room, narrowly avoiding a collision with Mary, who was bringing in Truthful's boiled eggs.

"He's actually Dutch, you know," said Lady Badgery. "Name of Kloppers. Known him for years. Nevertheless, a great artist in his chosen field."

"But why pretend to be Italian?" asked Truthful.

"People expect it, and pay more," said Lady Badgery. "There is a lesson there, Truthful. People adopt other personas for many different reasons, and there are more about than you might think."

"I'm sure," said Truthful, tapping her egg with a spoon in a desultory fashion that made no impact upon the shell.

"Do you regret your own masquerade as the chevalier?" asked Lady Badgery bluntly. "Though the Emerald has not yet been retrieved, it does seem likely that your efforts have seen to it that it will be, and the vile Plathenden will be brought to justice."

Truthful put down her spoon.

"I don't regret it," she said slowly. "I did what needed to be done. I even enjoyed some of it. But there are . . . aspects I wish would have turned out otherwise. I fear . . . I fear, Great-aunt, that I allowed myself to become too attached to Major Harnett."

"A handsome young man of considerable address, an adventure together, you barely out of the schoolroom," said Lady Badgery. "It is not to be surprised at, no, not at all."

"He made me an offer," said Truthful, addressing her egg rather than her great-aunt. "Because he said he had compromised me. But I asked him if he really *wanted* to marry me and he said no, he didn't want to marry anyone, and then last night I discover he is already *betrothed* and has been for some time."

"I see," said Lady Badgery, frowning. "I wasn't aware he had made you an offer and in such unfortunate terms! However, people do not always say what they really mean, and things are not always as they seem. In the case of Major Harnett—"

"Let us not speak of him," interrupted Truthful forcefully. "I know I have been foolish. I shall not think of him, or of any man! When the Emerald has been regained I will return to Newington Hall and stay there!"

"Hmph," said Lady Badgery, but even this monosyllabic expression was not without compassion. "Well, as you wish, Truthful. Shall we stay home this afternoon, or venture out?"

"Home," said Truthful. She took up her spoon again and fairly shattered the top of her egg. "Please let us stay home and be quiet."

"Very well," said Lady Badgery. "I will instruct Dworkin to deny us to *all* callers."

◆ ──ᴕ── ◆

This instruction kept Dworkin busy, for there were very many callers, most of them gentlemen wishing to visit Truthful and continue the acquaintance made at the ball the night before. However, one caller would not be denied, and made such a fuss of insisting upon entry that Lady Badgery herself came down to see what the commotion was about. Discovering it to be Mr. Stephen Newington-Lacy, she allowed him to be an exception and sent him on his way upstairs to see Truthful, who was reading *The Ladies' Monthly Museum* in her own small parlor.

She shrieked as Stephen entered without knocking, dropped her magazine, and rushed to embrace him.

"Stephen!"

"Now, now, no need to carry on," said the young man in disgusted tones, fending her off. "Anyone would think I was come back from the Indies with a leg missing."

"You *were* kidnapped," said Truthful.

"Oh, not for above five minutes," said Stephen. He laughed, his eyes sparkling. "But they were such slow-tops! Imagine not gagging me, so I could talk to the horses! They were happy enough to mount the gutter and overturn us, and then Charles's men were there and two watchmen came up, and before you know it, the boot was on the other foot! Though I am loathe to admit that one of them did escape. Not the one I held, I assure you."

"And then you simply joined in the search for Lady Plathenden, I collect?" asked Truthful, remembering the short and infuriating message from Harnett to that effect.

"Lord yes! I had the notion that a hound given the scent of a shoe the escaped rascal had shed in his flight might lead us to their lair. When I mentioned this, Charles asked me to assist in the matter, him not being as conversant with dogs and, of course, having no hounds to hand in the city. But I found a ratter name of Toby, with a nose like anything, and he did lead us to a kind of workman's shelter by the new canal tunnel under Maida Hill. Charles was most pleased. The occupants had fled but there was considerable evidence of their habitation and we hope clues as to other hideaways where Lady Plathenden might be found."

"You seem to have made great friends with Major Harnett," said Truthful easily, far more easily than she actually felt.

"Oh, Charles is a great gun," said Stephen, evidently having totally forgotten his first meeting with Major Harnett. "He suggested I stop in here before I go back to get the others, to let you know what is happening and to tell you that he has gone out of town. Following up what we discovered, you know."

"What do you mean 'to get the others'?" asked Truthful.

"Oh, Charles says he has not enough men and needs volunteers," said Stephen breezily. "I'm sure Edmund and Robert will jump at the chance. We'll be back tomorrow, I daresay, and we will be sure to call upon you, Newt."

"I am glad not to be forgotten amidst all your excitement," said Truthful tartly. "And where has Major Harnett's search taken him?"

"Brighton," said Stephen. He paused as Truthful gave a visible shiver. "Are you coming down with something?"

"No, no," said Truthful. "Go on."

"The rogues in the canal-house had several barrels from an inn there, the Black Lion, and Charles said he had seen another larger barrel somewhere else that was also connected with the matter."

"Oh," said Truthful, suddenly recalling the poker-work symbol on the barrel she had been imprisoned in. That could be a lion, squinted at in the right way. "I go to Brighton myself, on Wednesday. Perhaps I will be able to assist—"

"Best leave it to Charles," said Stephen. "He knows what he's about."

"Does he?" retorted Truthful angrily. "Do you know

where he'd be without my help?"

"No, I don't," said Stephen. "What do you mean?"

Truthful almost told him, but then that would mean a great many other explanations. Finally she shook her head and sighed. "Nothing, I suppose. But am I to understand from all this hustling about that Lady Plathenden is still not arrested?"

"Not yet," said Stephen, fixing her with his keen green eyes. "But is that all that disturbs you, Truthful?"

"No," said Truthful honestly. "But it isn't something you can help with, Stephen."

"I do like Charles, you know," said Stephen, unerringly and painfully striking at the point of Truthful's concerns. "I am sure Edmund and Robert will like him too. I mean, he's not a Duke, as we expected, but—"

"I don't know what you're talking about!" interrupted Truthful, her face burning up.

"Don't you?" asked Stephen in a very brotherly and unfeeling fashion. "Well, be like that! I must be off. I shall see you soon, I expect. Good-bye!"

With that, he turned on his heel, leaving Truthful feeling very much that she had not carried her side of the conversation at all well, and how difficult it would be if Major Harnett did indeed become friends with all her Newington-Lacy cousins.

"I shall have to go abroad," she whispered to herself, and her eyes filled with tears. She wiped them away and then suddenly laughed at the absurdity of her own words. Here she was, not two weeks in London, and already figuring herself as the lead player in an affecting tragedy! It was not to be borne. She drew herself up and recalled the words of Nelson that her father liked to declaim.

"The measure may be thought bold, but I am of the opinion the boldest are the safest."

Running away would do no good, Truthful decided. Rather she should take command of the situation and deny Harnett any opportunity to play with her affections. Going to her writing desk, she took pen and paper and wrote a short letter to him.

Dear Major Harnett,

    I am writing to wish you all happiness with Miss Gough, whom I had the pleasure of meeting at Lady Mournbeck's ball yestereve and who informed me of your long-standing betrothal. Given this intelligence, your most obliging offer to me must be considered a momentary aberration born of the unusual nature of our temporary situation. As your official position with regard to the continued pursuit of Lady Plathenden and the recovery of my Emerald means that we will be constrained to meet upon occasion in the future,

I must request that any communications between us

remain wholly to do with this official matter and shall

not stray into concerns of a personal nature. However,

I should like to be informed as soon as may be possible

on the exact detail of your investigation into my stolen

Emerald, where you suspect Lady Plathenden is now,

and your suspicions as to her future movements.

> *Yours etc.*

> *Lady Truthful Newington, at Badgery House*

Sealing her letter with a wafer, Truthful went downstairs and handed it to Dworkin.

"Have that Sergeant Ruggins send this to his master," said Truthful. "And I have changed my mind, Dworkin. I am at home this afternoon, and you may admit suitable callers to the blue saloon!"

17

UNSATISFACTORY CORRESPONDENCE

Determined to do her best not to languish, Truthful threw herself into a social whirl in the next several days and found that while it did not make her entirely forget Major Harnett, such dissipations as a silver loo party at which she won thirteen guineas; a card party at which she lost three dozen new sixpences; a daily walk in the park; a picnic in Box Hill; and entertaining a constant stream of mainly gentlemen callers did make the time pass more quickly and provided some hint that perhaps at some point in the future she would once again be able to take an unalloyed pleasure in such things.

A slight blemish was put upon these bright amusements by the continued presence of Sergeant Ruggins and her other guardians, who contrived to accompany her in all outings and were constantly about the house and the square. A greater blemish marred her enjoyment further in the shape of a belated note from Major Harnett, which did not arrive until Tuesday afternoon. It utterly failed to reply to Truthful's own letter, neglecting as it did to mention Miss Gough and his engagement at all and being rather vague about the pursuit of Lady Plathenden and the Emerald, in fact telling Truthful less than she had already gleaned from Stephen.

Dear Lady Truthful,

Lady Plathenden still eludes us, but we have reason to believe that she and the Emerald are hiding somewhere in the vicinity of Brighton. I have enlisted the assistance of your Newington-Lacy cousins, among other volunteers, the budget of our own department being not what it was during the times of War. I believe the danger to your person has lessened with Lady Plathenden being out of London, but as I understand you are shortly to remove to Brighton you must continue to be vigilant and your guard shall remain until such time as Lady Plathenden is securely in the Tower. Sergeant Ruggins may be relied on. He is considerably brighter than his appearance would indicate.

Yours etc.

"He hasn't signed it *again!*" said Truthful, throwing the letter down in disgust. "And he has been unkind about poor Sergeant Ruggins."

"The same poor Sergeant Ruggins who yesterday you declared was the greatest block alive when he wouldn't let you out of the house until the suspicious-looking flower sellers had departed the square?" asked Lady Badgery. She took up the letter and perused it, while Truthful had the grace to blush.

The two of them were in Lady Badgery's bedroom with Parkins, overseeing the packing of the dowager countess's clothes for Brighton, which in practice meant sitting together on the sofa reading letters and drinking orgeat while Parkins and one of the undermaids laid out various dresses on the bed and Lady Badgery indicated whether she wanted them to be taken on the expedition or not.

"It does explain why we haven't seen your Newington-Lacy cousins," said Lady Badgery. "I wonder if they will be at Otterbrook's Masquerade, since they are in Brighton."

"Why would they be?" asked Truthful, surprised. "Sir Robert might be acquainted with the Marquis, but I doubt any of the boys have ever met him."

"Perhaps they might run across each other," said Lady Badgery airily. "I daresay they would have many friends in common."

"I suppose them to be incognito, attempting to find Lady Plathenden," said Truthful. Her brow wrinkled. "I wonder how exactly they are going about the business?"

"Drinking in the Black Lion I would guess," said Lady Badgery. "No, not that one, Parkins."

"I should hope they have adopted some more scientific approach," said Truthful. She took up the next letter and opened it with Lady Badgery's Turkish dagger. "Here is Dr. Doyle's report. It seems Father is doing quite well compared with last week mutatis mutandis . . . really I have asked him time and time again not to put these things in Latin. I suppose he means there has been no change. Oh, I do wish I had the Emerald. Then Father would be well, and I could have no more to do with . . . with such difficult matters."

Lady Badgery nodded, possibly in agreement. Parkins laid the final dress out, which was greeted with a scowl and a definitively negative wave of the hand.

"Parkins will see to your dresses now," said Lady Badgery. "And I shall have a nap. Signor Fraticelli has promised our costumes by six o'clock. We shall dine in tonight, for tomorrow we must leave very early. I do not like traveling in the heat of the day."

"Yes, Great-aunt," said Truthful dutifully.

It took little more than an hour for Parkins and her assistant to pack Truthful's clothes. But when they were done, and dismissed, Truthful went to the locked chest by the foot of her bed and took out several other articles. These she bundled together in a cloak and put at the bottom of the larger case: the shirt, breeches, coat, hat, and top boots of a country gentleman; her spare corset; a box with two pocket pistols, powder, and shot; and in a snuffbox, her ensorcelled moustache.

The drive to Brighton was a pleasant one, but it was not fast. There was no danger that Lady Badgery's procession would come anywhere near Sir John Lade's record run from London to the coastal town. In fact, it was a full eight hours after they set out near dawn that Lady Badgery's modern and comfortable post chaise and four clattered along the Marine Parade. It was followed by two older coaches: the first for Dworkin, Parkins, and some lesser servants, and the second entirely loaded or even overloaded with luggage. The whole convoy was accompanied not only by Sergeant Ruggins and his four men on horseback but also three of Lady Badgery's grooms.

Lord Otterbrook's house was as he described, an extremely large residence four floors in height and a frontage featuring two front doors, with a stable yard and some gardens behind. The house commanded an excellent view across the Parade, the curiously reddish pebbled beach, and the sea beyond.

Truthful and Lady Badgery were welcomed by the Marchioness, who apologized for the absence of the Marquis, who she said "was somewhere about the town." After they had seen their comfortable rooms in the "right-hand house" as she called it, the "left-hand house" apparently being reserved for male guests, she offered them refreshments, which Lady Badgery accepted. Truthful declined, instead requesting that she might be allowed to walk to the Steine and look upon the Pavilion, which she had only glimpsed from the carriage window as they passed.

This was allowed, a maid being directed to follow her, along with Sergeant Ruggins and one of his cohorts. Truthful quickly supervised the unpacking of her cases, taking care to squirrel away one particular package, and changed her rather dull traveling dress of dove gray muslin for a more fetching promenade dress of pale green with a tall collar, matched with a charming merino coat in a darker shade of green with saffron edges and silver-buttoned epaulettes, topped with a charming straw bonnet adorned with a silver ribbon. Thus equipped to enrapture the gaze of gentlemen and attract the envy of gentlewomen, she went out into the street.

A strong sea wind was blowing in from the southwest, which threatened her bonnet, at least until they turned into the Steine, where some shelter was offered by the surrounding buildings, even though it was quite a large open space, indicative of its origins as the green it had once been. Truthful, who had studied her guidebook, noted Steine House, the residence of Mrs. Fitzherbert, but she was intent on making her way to the Marine Pavilion some little way off. This appeared smaller to her than she expected, though the large dome of the stables behind it was impressive, and she supposed it would be a grander building when the work that was currently in train was finished. At present there was a kind of iron scaffold going up around the small dome in the center of the building, and a great many workmen were engaged in making a mess of the ground about the place. All in all, it was quite disappointing.

However, a view of the Pavilion was not Truthful's main object.

"Where would I find the Black Lion Inn?" she asked Sergeant Ruggins, who was as usual surveying anyone who came within ten feet of her with a suspicious gaze.

"You don't want to go there, milady," said Ruggins. He pointed to the mass of closely set buildings to the south and west of the Pavilion. "In them narrow lanes, anything could happen."

"I see," said Truthful. "Very well. We shall go back."

The return walk took a little longer, as Truthful encountered several people she knew who could not be ignored, unseasonably in Brighton for the Otterbrook's ball. One was the unfortunate Mr. Trellingsworth, who had become emboldened by Truthful's kindness at Lady Mournbeck's ball and was fair to becoming a nuisance. Luckily he soon found that the shade of his green coat and green pantaloons clashed with Truthful's own green ensemble, so he had to regretfully deny himself the privilege of walking with her.

On Truthful's return she discovered both the Marchioness and the dowager countess had retired to recoup their energy before dinner, which was to be served at the compromise time between city and country hours of seven o'clock. Truthful yawned and declared to Parkins that she also would take advantage of a short nap, and there was no need for anyone to attend to her until half an hour before the appointed hour to dine.

But Truthful did not take to her bed. Instead she carefully dressed in her masculine attire, affixed her moustache, loaded her pistols, and put them in the pockets of her driving coat. Then, disarraying her hair with clawed fingers, she pulled her hat down on her head and crept through the house to the stables at the rear, narrowly avoiding two of the maids.

As she had expected, one of Harnett's men was watching

the gate, and there were two grooms in the stable yard. Truthful considered them for several seconds, wondering how she could get past. One leaf of the gate was open, but the guard stood smack-bang in the middle, and there was no way of crossing the yard without being seen by the grooms.

As she was pondering this problem, her eyes ran across the horse-boxes, and stopped as she saw one very familiar bay mare. But what on earth was Stephen's horse doing here?

Truthful pursed her lips and wondered if she was going mad. The white patch was very distinctive, but there had to be at least a slim possibility that some other horse might have the same one.

She dismissed this puzzle, as looking at the horses had given her an idea. Watching the men carefully, she quickly ducked out from her cover by the door, slid back the bolts fastening the closest horse-box, and retreated to the shadows again.

The mare inside, a riding hack of no great nobility, watched as the gate of her box slowly swung open. But she did not take advantage of this freedom, flicking her ears instead in irritation or even fear at this unlooked-for motion.

"Oh, you silly animal," whispered Truthful. "Walk on. Walk on!"

Whether the horse heard Truthful's whisper or felt some of her magic, she did step out of the box. And stopped again, lowering her head to snatch up some fallen straw.

"Go!" whispered Truthful. "Make a fuss!"

The horse blinked and twitched her ears again. Seeing another swath of straw, she idled over to it, but this time her hooves rang clear on the cobbled floor—finally catching the attention of the grooms.

"Here, Christie's out!" called one. He came walking quickly back, his companion at his heels.

"Wolves!" whispered Truthful, investing her words with power. "Bears! Donkeys and wild dogs!"

Christie's amiability disappeared at once. She reared violently, sending both grooms flying back on their behinds. As they struggled to get up, the mare dashed between them, heading for the open gate. The guard there, no coward, stood his ground until the last second, and snatched at the horse's halter as she passed. Catching it, he was dragged through the gateway and off, cursing and bellowing for assistance.

Truthful ran past the grooms, calling out, "Hold on!" as gruffly as she could manage. But once past the gate, she turned left, where horse and guard had bolted right toward the seafront.

Walking briskly with her head down and one hand clapped on her hat to keep it in place, Truthful was soon back at the Steine. Cutting across it, she entered the narrow lanes of the old town and began to look for the Black Lion.

It was darker here where the buildings crowded together, and the people were not at all of the quality to be found promenading about the Steine. But Truthful was relieved to notice they were generally respectable citizens. This was an area of some industry, with shops and workshops in abundance and much business being done. Truthful particularly noticed a tinsmith, a bakery that smelled quite wonderful, and a shop full of the most interesting wooden toys.

And at last, there was the Black Lion. Truthful paused to eye the battered hanging sign and was considering whether she should enter or not when a hand suddenly gripped her elbow with considerable force.

"Stephen!" hissed a familiar voice close to her ear. "What are you doing! You mustn't be seen here dressed like that!"

18

A SIGHTING IN BRIGHTON

Truthful turned around, the grip lessening, and came face-to-face with Major Harnett. Not the ink-stained writer of Paternoster Row or the elegant gentleman of White's. Not even the sodden survivor of his bowsprit experience. This was Harnett as a common laborer, his face dirty, his coat of some cloth a close cousin to a sack, and his trousers truly unmentionable.

"By God!" he said, his grip once again tightening. "No!"

"Unhand me!" croaked Truthful, struggling against his grip.

Surprisingly, Harnett let go. Even more surprisingly,

he truckled low and tugged his forelock, at the same time speaking urgently in a whisper.

"Tru . . . damn it, you are in great danger! Follow me, I beg you!"

Truthful hesitated for a moment. Harnett looked up at her, and she saw fear in his eyes. Fear for her, she realized with a pang. Nodding her head, she indicated she would follow. Harnett immediately led her down the narrow lane, around a corner, and into the doorway of a modest tea merchant's shop. The door opened at once. Harnett rushed in, and Truthful followed.

A man in a shopkeeper's garb slid a pistol back into the front pocket of his green apron and stood aside. Harnett nodded to him, took Truthful by the elbow, and led her upstairs. Passing the doorway of a chamber on the second floor, Truthful saw a man looking out between the curtains of the window there into the lane, down at the front entrance of the Black Lion.

"Anything?" asked Harnett, pausing.

The man shook his head. Harnett nodded and led Truthful up to an empty chamber on the third floor, which also overlooked the lane, the curtains similarly drawn to create a narrow viewing aperture. A chair set by it indicated the position of another watcher, though it was currently not occupied.

As soon as they were in this room and the door shut, Harnett exploded.

"I will break Ruggins for this! You could have been killed! What were you thinking?"

"I thought I was merely to be in danger of kidnapping," sniffed Truthful. "In which case I would hope you to rescue me."

"Not if you are presumed to be Stephen," said Harnett, his face set. "Plathenden doesn't need *him*, and she knows he is working with me."

"Oh," said Truthful. She hadn't thought of that. "I just wanted . . . you were taking so long, and I *must* recover the Emerald!"

"Can you not leave well enough alone?" asked Harnett in exasperated tones. "If you had gone into that tavern . . . a knife in your back . . ."

"Well, I did not go in," said Truthful. "And I have not got a knife in my back. Is Lady Plathenden in there?"

"Not yet," said Harnett. "But we have proven she owns the place, and she has been seen in Brighton. That is why we are 'taking so long'! We must watch and wait, here and two other houses where she may turn up. One such watch is by your cousins, in the guise of clay-diggers, which is why I had the terrible shock of seeing Stephen Newington-Lacy attired as a gentleman expressly against my orders and, not only that, simply strolling up to the Black Lion as if he had not a care in the world!"

"I am sorry," said Truthful. "But if you simply *told* me what was going on I wouldn't need to investigate for myself!"

"I will have to send for Sergeant Ruggins to escort you to your lodgings, as soon as I may," said Harnett heavily. "We are devilishly shorthanded. But once home, I trust you will assume your . . . your feminine identity and stay safe!"

"I don't wish to stay safe," said Truthful. She strode over to the chair and sat down, twitching the curtain aside. "I can watch too!"

Harnett clenched his fists but did not immediately answer. Truthful snatched one glance at him, then set her face toward the lane below.

"Truthful, I know I have been angry with you, unwarrantably so. We have been at odds and misunderstood each other," said Harnett, speaking slowly and with obvious effort to stay calm. "But please hear me. Lady Plathenden is a very dangerous woman, of great resource. She leads a large number of men, and women too, who will stop at nothing to do her bidding. She is a malignant sorcerer, and you are at great risk from her. If she has not yet mastered the Emerald then she will want you to help further her aims. If she has, then she will want you dead in order to have no rival for its powers. So you must go where you will be safe!"

Truthful showed no sign of hearing his words. She was staring intently out the window at a caped figure, a short woman with her hood up and a hatbox on her hip who had emerged from the doorway of the Black Lion. She couldn't see her face, but there was something about the way she walked . . .

"It's her!" she exclaimed, pointing so hard her fingernail scratched against the glass.

"Plathenden!" exclaimed Harnett, leaping forward to see.

"No," said Truthful. "My maid! Agatha!"

"I must go after her," said Harnett. "Stay here!"

Truthful waited for two seconds, then disobeyed, following him as he went clattering down the stairs in a rush, calling out to his men.

"Keep watch for Plathenden!"

Harnett didn't even notice Truthful until he was outside and the door shut behind them both. He was craning on tiptoe to see over the heads of the crowd and staggered as Truthful ran into him.

"Can you never do as you are told!" he snapped. "Stay by me!"

With that, he slid between two large meat carriers and slipped past a woman carrying a bag of potatoes almost her own size. Truthful followed as closely as she could at his heels, ducking and weaving, jumping up whenever opportunity allowed to catch sight of Agatha, always some twenty or thirty bobbing heads in front of them.

Finally the lane joined a somewhat broader street that ran up the hill and down to the seafront. Harnett paused by the corner of a house there, his head turning swiftly from left to right. Obviously he had lost their quarry. Truthful was just catching up to him when she saw the air shimmer behind him and to his side, and Agatha appeared out of the whitewashed wall, a stone knife in her hand.

"Charles!" screamed Truthful in her true voice. At the same time she reached for a pistol, but the lock caught on the edge of the pocket of her coat, and she could not get it free.

Harnett whirled about and caught Agatha's wrist, turning the knife aside so it scraped across his shoulder rather than plunging in his heart. He twisted harder and Agatha dropped the knife. But she did not surrender, instead raking at Harnett's face with her left hand, the nails there suddenly grown long and sharp. He grabbed that wrist also, and the two of them struggled violently from side to side, Harnett shocked at finding his strength matched by a lady's maid, Agatha's face twisted in fury.

Truthful finally got her pistol free. Cocking the lock, she levelled it at Agatha's back and after the briefest moment of consideration, pulled the trigger. There was a resounding crack, a great plume of white smoke, and then, much to

240

Truthful's surprise, something whizzed past her own ear with a whistling cry.

The ball had somehow ricocheted off Agatha's back!

"The bracelet!" shouted Harnett. "Touch her with the bracelet!"

Truthful had forgotten she was wearing the gold and silver wire bracelet, it was so slim. Dropping the empty pistol, she slid back her coat cuff and struck Agatha hard in the middle of her back.

"It's not touching!" roared Harnett, who was slowly being overborn by the unnatural strength of the ferocious Agatha. "Pull your shirtsleeve up as well!"

Truthful struggled to push her shirt cuff back and bring the bracelet forward, unfortunately tangling immediately with her cuff links.

"Hurry!" gasped Harnett. He was down on one knee and Agatha's talons were almost plucking at his eyes. "Hurry!"

"I am hurrying!" shrieked Truthful. At last she got the bracelet clear and pressed her wrist hard against Agatha's back. She didn't know what would happen, but the last thing she expected was for the woman to utter an unearthly scream and collapse at her feet, quite dead.

"Part fay at the least," gasped Harnett, struggling to his feet. "Stone Nymph, I suppose."

Stone Nymphs were the most inimical of the faery folks,

holding humans in great enmity.

"I didn't know," said Truthful slowly. She stared down at her former maid's body. Agatha's skin was already darkening to a stony gray. For some reason her eyes found it hard to focus. "I never really knew anything about her. . . ."

Harnett picked up the empty pistol and looked about them. The crowd was silent now, everyone stopped, all business halted. All eyes were upon Harnett and Truthful and the body on the ground, still leaking the hideous, tarry substance that was the equivalent of fay blood. Harnett bent down, picked up the hatbox Agatha had been carrying, and thrust it into Truthful's hands.

"You must go! Take this with you. Fast as you can. I will wait for the constables and will follow when I may. Please, this once, do as I ask!"

He pushed her in the middle of her back. With a start, Truthful set off down the street. A great murmur rose up behind her, and she heard someone cry, "Murder!" and then Harnett calling out in clear, commanding tones.

"I am a government officer! Someone send for the constable, and be about your business!"

Truthful kept walking. The street zigzagged so that when she glanced over her shoulder she could no longer see Harnett, but could only hear the roar of the crowd and gauge its feeling from that sound. She felt desperately frightened, but not for herself. If the mob took it upon itself to have a lynching, there was Harnett alone . . .

Help must be dispatched, Truthful thought. At once! Still clutching the hatbox, she began to run as she had never run before, not even stopping when her hat blew off as she rounded the corner to the seafront and emerged into the southwesterly breeze.

A scant six minutes later, one of Harnett's men on guard outside the Otterbrook's right-hand front door saw a young gentleman carrying a hatbox come charging toward him, his driving coat flying open and no hat on his head.

"Halt or I shoot!" the guard shouted, drawing his pistol.

19

SURPRISING REVELATIONS
FROM CURIOUS QUARTERS

Truthful slowed, fell to one knee, and dropped the hatbox. The lid came off and rolled against the lower step.

"Call Sergeant Ruggins!" she gasped. "At once!"

"You stay where you are," ordered the nervous guard, looking down at the red hair of this strange, but also strangely familiar, young gentleman. He backed up the steps and knocked upon the door. The porter inside, already alert to some peculiar circumstance, opened it a crack.

"Thank . . . you," said Truthful, just managing to get the words out between great gulps of air. "I am . . . Chevalier de

Vienne . . . Lady Truthful's cousin. Please tell . . . Lady Badgery I am here."

The guard and the porter exchanged a swift look.

"Better call Sergeant Ruggins from the stables," said the guard. "And tell Mr. Dworkin."

The porter frowned, but disappeared back inside.

The guard kept his eye on Truthful, and the pistol was still in his hand. That hand twitched as she dragged the hatbox closer and looked inside.

There was a hat in it, which she didn't expect. Or not exactly a hat, but a kind of helmet designed to completely enclose the head, a papier-mâché thing of sea green with silver scales and fishy appendages at the sides in place of ears.

"Chevalier?"

Truthful looked up. Sergeant Ruggins was at the door. He too had his pistol by his side.

"Sergeant Ruggins! Major Harnett may be in danger from a mob," exclaimed Truthful, only at the last second remembering to pitch her voice low, so her first words came out as a squeak. "He is where a lane comes out on Ship Street, near a butcher's. Please, you must send help!"

"Stay where you are," ordered Sergeant Ruggins. His tone was not at all like it was when he usually spoke to Truthful.

"You must send help!" demanded Truthful.

"We'll look into it," said Ruggins. He moved down a step

to let someone else look out the door, glancing back over his shoulder. "Ah, milady. Is that who I think it is?"

"Yes, it is my cousin, Henri de Vienne," said Lady Badgery calmly. "You should have told us you were planning to visit, my boy. Come inside."

"Major Harnett," gasped Truthful once again. She picked up the hatbox and staggered to her feet.

"I'll send men," said Ruggins. "Before I do, was that you who . . . ah . . . caused the commotion in the stables some half an hour ago . . . sir?"

"Yes, yes," agreed Truthful. "Only hurry. Major Harnett . . . the crowd, a lynch mob!"

"In Brighton?" asked Lady Badgery. "I doubt it, Chevalier. You live too out of the world to understand an English crowd. Come with me."

That last command was said very sternly. Truthful bowed her head and followed, aware that she had put herself in the position of earning a terrible scold from her great-aunt. But Truthful hardly cared, she was so relieved that Lady Badgery thought Harnett was in no danger.

This feeling lasted only until she got inside and found Lady Otterbrook coming down the grand stairs to see what the commotion was at her front door. All of a sudden the likelihood of being found out struck her, and she would have turned and fled if her great-aunt had not such a strong hold on her elbow.

"Lucy. This is my cousin the Chevalier Henri de Vienne, the young man I told you about."

Truthful looked sharply at Lady Badgery, who ignored her.

"Make your bow to Lady Otterbrook, Chevalier," she said.

Truthful obeyed automatically, almost emptying the contents of the hatbox by accident as she did so.

"We are going to take a dish of tea in the parlor you so kindly allowed me," said Lady Badgery. "And catch up on family gossip. Then I fear the chevalier has an engagement in . . . in Portsmouth and must ride on."

"Alas," said Lady Otterbrook. "Can you not stay to dine, Chevalier?"

"I fear not, my lady," said Truthful gruffly. "I am spoken for . . . ah . . . elsewhere."

"Never mind," declared the Marchioness. "Oh, Ermintrude, if you should see Lady Truthful, I would be glad to drink a glass of ratafia with her before dinner, in my own parlor."

"I will tell her," said Lady Badgery. "She will be delighted!"

Truthful sent her a horrified glance, but again Lady

Badgery ignored her, pushing her along and up the great staircase. As they passed Lady Otterbrook, the two old ladies bowed and Truthful, clumsily bowing a moment too late, thought she detected the slight quirk of a smile in the corner of the Marchioness's mouth.

Inside the saloon, Lady Badgery settled herself comfortably on the sofa and patted the cushion next to her invitingly. Truthful sat woodenly, the hatbox in her lap.

"What have you been doing now?" asked Lady Badgery. She did not sound angry, only curious.

"I killed Agatha!" said Truthful, and burst into tears. "I touched her with my bracelet and she died! Major Harnett said she was a Stone Nymph, not human at all!"

"Oh," said Lady Badgery, considerably taken aback. "Did you become the chevalier in order to kill Agatha?"

"No, no," sobbed Truthful. "I didn't know she was here. I just wanted to do something, to help find the Emerald, and no one would let me! And now I am a murderess!"

"You are not a murderess!" snapped Lady Badgery. "I do not suppose you meant Agatha to die?"

"I shot her with a pistol first, only the ball bounced off her," said Truthful. "But she would have killed Major Harnett!"

"Ah," said Lady Badgery. "Major Harnett is involved."

"Yes," said Truthful. "He was trying to arrest her, but she hid in a wall and then came out with a knife, and then such talons—"

"Clearly it was very necessary to kill her," said Lady Badgery.

"I suppose so," said Truthful, her sobs slowing. "But it is a most awful feeling, Great-aunt, you cannot imagine."

"On the contrary," said Lady Badgery comfortably. "I have killed dozens of people."

"Dozens!"

"I am not sure of the exact number," mused Lady Badgery. She hesitated, then said crossly, "I suppose I must tell you all my secrets. But they are not to be shared, understand, not with anyone. Not even with your Major Harnett."

"He is not my Major Harnett," said Truthful, new tears welling up despite her best efforts to dash them away. "He is Miss Gough's, and I am only crying because of the shock of killing Agatha."

"I know, dear," said Lady Badgery. "As to the impressive score of deaths that may be laid at my door, they all occurred in the six years I lived as a man in the Army, as a lieutenant to my beloved Badgery. All were in battle, you understand. Oh, there was one duel, but that was an accident. I barely nicked him but he later died of an infection."

249

Truthful had stopped crying at the phrase "six years I lived as a man" and was staring at her great-aunt, her green eyes very wide indeed.

"You lived as a man?" she asked, incredulous.

Lady Badgery smiled.

"We were just married, and Badgery was sent to America to fight the French and then the rebels," she said. "He did not want to leave me behind, and I did not want to be left. I could not accompany him as his wife, so I went as his lieutenant. It was a most instructive time. Remember I told you that there were many reasons people may adopt a masquerade?"

"No one ever guessed?" asked Truthful.

"Some people may have guessed, but they held their tongues," said Lady Badgery. She had a faraway look in her eyes, and a pensive smile. "In our day Badgery and I were sorcerers of the first order, and together our glamours were all but impenetrable, extending even to . . . well, they were extremely durable, shall we say?"

A thought suddenly crossed Truthful's mind, a most terrifying thought, even more so than picturing Lady Badgery as a young lieutenant.

"Hasn't Parkins been with you since you were married?" she asked.

Lady Badgery smiled again.

"Sergeant *Harkins* she was in those days," she said. "She

had the most remarkable beard. I wonder if she still has it. We must ask her one day. But enough of these maudlin recollections of times long past. Tell me exactly what has happened, and then you must return to being Lady Truthful and go to Lady Otterbrook. She has something of importance to tell you, I believe."

"I don't understand," said Truthful. "I hardly know . . . surely it is not about the time Lord Otterbrook forced my coach from the road? He did offer to take me up in his curricle, but he quickly apologized when he realized it would not do. . . ."

"No, it is not that," said Lady Badgery. "But tell me what has occurred! And why do you have a mermaid's head in that hatbox? Your Diana costume is far more becoming."

"Oh, it is not mine," said Truthful. "Agatha had it. I can't imagine it was her own, either. Look, there are real emeralds among the scales . . ."

She faltered in mid-speech, her mind racing.

"Lady Plathenden! She must plan to go to the Masquerade Ball, disguised as a mermaid!"

"Possible," mused Lady Badgery. "It is true that she always loved a masked ball and other opportunities for costume. But why would she wish to attend this particular Masquerade?"

"The Prince Regent," suggested Truthful doubtfully. "Perhaps she wishes to assassinate him? After all, wasn't her husband executed by the Crown? Stephen said that was the case."

"Lord Plathenden was found guilty of murder by necromancy and other crimes of malignant sorcery in a court of law and was subsequently executed. But the presiding judge was Lord Elphinmore, and he is still alive and besides, doesn't attend balls. I suppose she could hold a grudge against the government . . . but then she would be more likely to want to assassinate the prime minister, I would expect. Like poor Mr. Perceval. But I cannot think Lady Plathenden would have any particular hatred for Lord Liverpool. I doubt he will be at the Masquerade, in any case. So she must be up to something else. Doubtless nothing good."

"Can you scry her purpose?" asked Truthful.

Lady Badgery shook her head.

"You forget she has the Emerald. It clouds all such divination. But I suspect you may be right. We must apprise Major . . . we must inform the appropriate authorities that the Prince Regent may be in danger, and to beware a mermaid at the ball. Though I daresay Amelia will change her costume now she is lacking the head. But once again we have strayed from the point. Tell me what happened, Truthful!"

By the time Truthful had finished answering Lady Badgery's questions she only just had time to become herself again before the dreaded engagement with Lady Otterbrook. However, she did manage to dash downstairs and ask the guard at the front door for news of Harnett, and was relieved when he professed no knowledge of any danger to his superior and offered his opinion that all was as expected it should be.

This relief did not last long as she ascended the stairs and knocked on the door of Lady Otterbrook's parlor. Rack her brains as she might, she could not think of any reason why the august Marchioness would want to speak to her.

Nor did Lady Otterbrook immediately inform her, the tension thus building. She offered Truthful ratafia, which she accepted, and spoke some commonplaces about Brighton, which Truthful returned.

Only after some ten minutes of excruciating anticipation did Lady Otterbrook broach the main subject she wished to disclose to Truthful.

"You may wonder why I wished to speak to you, child," she said. "I do not wonder at it, for it is not anything in the usual way."

Truthful nodded, not daring to speak. She was mortally afraid that Lady Otterbrook was going to denounce her for her masquerade and become instrumental in having her cast out of society. Not that she cared about that, as she intended to retreat to Newington House in any case, and care for her father in his declining years. But it would be very embarrassing.

"My nephew," said Lady Otterbrook, "appears to have made a complete mull of the matter, and your great-aunt Ermintrude and I have agreed that enough is enough and so I must step in."

"Your nephew?" asked Truthful in a puzzled tone.

"My nephew," said Lady Otterbrook with a sigh. "I should explain that when he was eighteen he fell most passionately in love with Arabella Thornton. This would be just before the truce of '03, you understand. I expect you have read or heard about Arabella Thornton?"

"No," said Truthful, now completely at a loss.

"They were to be married that September," said Lady Otterbrook, sighing again. "My nephew and Miss Thornton. But then, three days before the wedding, she ran off."

"Ran off?"

"With a Frenchman!" declared Lady Otterbrook. "Apparently she had been conducting an *affaire* with him since the previous May. From that time on, my nephew has been perhaps understandably . . . brittle . . . when it comes to women pretending to be other than they are, and also very distrustful of Frenchmen."

"I don't understand," said Truthful. "Are you speaking of Major Harnett? How could he be your nephew?"

"I think perhaps he had best explain that to you himself," said Lady Otterbrook. She rose to her feet and went to

254

the door, opening it. "I will leave you with him for five minutes. That should suffice."

"No, no, Your Grace!" protested Truthful, her face going almost as red as her hair. "It isn't proper. What would Miss Gough think?"

"Charles?" asked Lady Otterbrook, allowing Major Harnett to enter before she swept out.

"I am not acquainted with Miss Gough," said Charles, bowing to Truthful. He was no longer in sackcloth, but was once again the elegant gentleman, though Truthful barely noticed the superb cut of his deep blue coat or the extreme whiteness of his knee breeches and stockings, her eyes going immediately to his handsome face. He looked a little anxious, which prevented Truthful from immediately responding to his outrageous comment.

"I am not acquainted with Miss Gough," repeated Charles, "because I am not in fact Major Harnett—"

"What?" shrieked Truthful. Realizing the volume of her shout, she clapped her hands over her mouth and her eyebrows went up in dismay.

"I am actually Charles Otterbrook, Colonel the Viscount Lytchett," continued Charles. "As I have been trying to tell you for some time!"

THE MAKING OF PLANS

"I would like to make your acquaintance afresh, Lady Truthful," said Lord Lytchett, bowing over the hand that she had unconsciously raised to him. He kissed it and added, "And present my apologies for the deception that I initially undertook in the belief that you were a French agent."

"I understand," said Truthful stiffly. "Your aunt has explained."

Lord Lytchett blushed, a curious sight that Truthful had not seen before but found quite charming and made her wholly unbend. She felt she must now have become very pale herself and close to fainting, her thoughts and feelings as wild as the sea beyond the window, so churned up she was not exactly sure what was uppermost. A sudden, unexpected joy, coupled with annoyance and topped with excitement . . .

"I must also thank you for saving my life. Again," said Lord Lytchett. "And beg you to join with my officers tonight after dinner to discuss our plans for the capture of Lady Plathenden."

"Really?" asked Truthful, clapping her hands. Excitement was definitely winning out.

"I have learned my lesson," said Lord Lytchett. "And I have been spoken to by your great-aunt. As the Chevalier de Vienne or as Lady Truthful, I think you must be part of any action we take to reclaim your Emerald. Indeed, as all our success to date can be laid at your door, it shall be as you asked in your last letter. No details will be kept from you."

"Thank you," said Truthful. She hesitated, wanting to ask him whether everything would be as in her last letter, where she had asked they meet on business only. But she was suddenly shy, not knowing how to approach him now that he was to some degree a new person, almost a stranger.

Lord Lytchett seemed to have something of the same feeling, for he opened his mouth to speak but nothing came out. He frowned a little and glanced at the window. Truthful glanced at the window too, and sought desperately for something to say.

"I believe it will be fine for the ball tomorrow," she said, after the silence had stretched for what felt like minutes, but was probably only seconds.

"I . . . ah . . . believe it may even be quite warm," said Lord Lytchett. He took a deep breath, looked back at Truthful, and said, "I hope you will stand up with me for a dance at the Masquerade?"

"Won't you be busy?" asked Truthful, looking up at him through her eyelashes. "Looking out for Lady Plathenden?"

"I . . . will be mingling to some degree, I expect," said Lord Lytchett. His blush came back a little as he said, "Perhaps we might even waltz . . . we will be masked and it is Brighton, so perhaps—"

"Oh!" interrupted Truthful. "Charles, I had forgotten! There was a mermaid's head in Agatha's hatbox!"

"A mermaid's head?" asked Charles. He made the connection immediately. "A costume? I must see it!"

Truthful took his hand.

"It's in my great-aunt's parlor. If we hurry there will be just time before dinner."

She opened the door, surprising Lady Otterbrook, who was about to come in. Seeing Truthful's hand clasped in her nephew's, she exclaimed, "Oh, wonderful!"

"What?" asked Charles. He looked down at Truthful's hand and released it, just as she reluctantly withdrew it herself. "Oh, ah . . . we're off to look at a mermaid's head. And it is all right to combine the dinners!"

"Combine the dinners?" asked Truthful.

"Left-hand and right-hand houses," said Charles. "I wasn't sure . . . that is, if you didn't wish to hear me out . . . the fact of the matter is I have your cousins staying here. And the real Major Harnett. My friend James. His book is finished and I have recruited him to join our efforts against Lady Plathenden."

"Oh, I am pleased his book is done," exclaimed Truthful. "Now he and Miss Gough can marry."

"He is a capital fellow and I wish him very happy," said Charles. "I am also in his debt for allowing me to assume his identity when we first met, particularly as so much of his manuscript was damaged."

"Why did you?" asked Truthful. "Why not simply be yourself?"

"Well, I . . . we . . . had thought you were a French spy, and I am not unknown as a hunter of the same," said Charles. Catching sight of the hatbox he quickly changed the subject. "Is that the head? Very fancy. Those are small emeralds, are they not? It must be for Lady Plathenden herself."

"That is exactly what I said to my great aunt," said Truthful.

They beamed at each other, pleased at their mutual intelligence.

"So she intends to go to the Masquerade," mused Charles. "It must be for some fell purpose. . . . We have to tell Uncle. He had best warn off the Prince Regent."

"My thought exactly," cried Truthful.

"It will be one less thing to concern us," said Charles. "The thing is, if she is going to come to the Masquerade, she will certainly have the Emerald on her person. She may intend to use it, in which case you will be one of the few who might be able to resist its powers. And there lies our opportunity."

"Our opportunity?" asked Truthful.

"We will finally know exactly where Lady Plathenden and the Emerald are located," said Charles. "And we can capture both at one fell swoop!"

"I trust it proves as simple as that," said Lady Badgery from the door. "I will be very surprised if it does. But now we must go downstairs. The dinner gong has sounded twice, and Otterbrook is very tedious when he's famished!"

The dinner, combining the ladies of the right-hand house with the menfolk of the left-hand house, was a jubilant affair.

Truthful was greeted by her cousins with exuberant tales of their activities in pursuit of Lady Plathenden and her many accomplices interspersed with apologies from Edmund and Robert for not, after all, going to get her new gemstones as they had promised in their cups. She was delighted to meet the rather shy Major Harnett, and promised that she would buy copies of his *Badajoz Diary* for everyone she knew, and wished him very happy with Miss Gough. The Marquis, informed of the possibility of Lady Plathenden somehow attacking his guests, seemed rather more pleased than otherwise and had to be constrained by Lady Otterbrook from having another look in his divining fire just in case he could get a glimpse of what might occur.

After the last remove, when it would have been normal for the ladies to retire, the whole company instead moved to the library, where Charles laid out everything that was known about Lady Plathenden's activities in Brighton, the smugglers, pickpockets, and other criminal riffraff who served her, and the forces of the Crown that might be arrayed for the purposes of her apprehension and the reclamation of the Emerald.

Much discussion was then to be had on the necessity of calling up the militia, the marines from Portsmouth, or even the Sorcery-Eaters of the Tower, but in the end it was decided that Harnett's existing force of a dozen men and the local constabulary—who had already been drafted in by the Marquis to manage the traffic expected to congregate around the Assembly Rooms of the Old Ship—would suffice, particularly as General Leye was posting down the next morning and would bring half a dozen more men with him and the Sorcerer-Royal, Sir Everard Loraine.

The Prince Regent also had his own guards, but as they would remain with him in the Pavilion, they did not enter into the plans other than in the necessity of informing their commander of what was going forward, the Marquis indicating that he would ensure this was done, while also speaking with the Prince Regent so he would not venture out and put himself at risk.

It was further decided that while the Newington-Lacys and Major Harnett would remain outside the Assembly Rooms, with their horses nearby in case a pursuit became necessary, Truthful and Charles would go to the Masquerade, it being easier for them as guests to survey the interior than in any other guise.

"I will be there also," said Lady Badgery. "With cutlass and wand! If Amelia Plathenden comes within lunging distance, I won't answer for the consequence."

"Thank you, milady," said Charles gravely. "Let us hope we can capture her alive."

"Is any more known about what she may be able to do

with the Emerald?" asked Truthful. "As far as I know, it was only ever used to raise or quell storms in my family, and that seems of little use for a malignant sorcerer of Lady Plathenden's ilk. General Leye said that it may have far greater elemental powers."

"We know little more," said Charles. "Sir Everard may, when he arrives. He has been searching the archives. General Leye was perturbed to see a report on an emerald that matches the description of the Newington gem in a very old inventory found with the Canterbury codex."

"The Canterbury codex?" asked Stephen, with a whistle. "Lore!"

"What is the Canterbury codex?" asked Truthful.

"A book of spells and other lore compiled for King Canute," answered Stephen excitedly. "I wonder if his power over the tides came from the Emerald?"

"I suppose it is possible," said Charles. He frowned, then shook his head. "Surely if it was, it would have been better known and would have been mentioned in some of the later royal tomes. I can't see the first William letting such a thing fall from his hand when he conquered England."

"Speaking of Canute," said the Marquis. "Prinny didn't like the idea of dressing up as him. So I decided to take it on myself. Must go and practice with the footmen who are going to be my waves."

"Oh, Athelstan!" said the Marchioness. "I cannot like this notion. Just think of how much space they will take up. They will be forever getting in the way!"

"Nonsense!" replied the Marquis. "I'll have a throne put up in the northeast corner, keep 'em there. Bit of fun, hey?"

He rose to his feet, advised all present not to drink too much before going into action as it were tomorrow, and left. He was soon followed by his wife and Lady Badgery, who in her turn offered the advice that everyone should stay close at home before the Masquerade, though her particular stare at Truthful made it clear who she thought most needed her counsel.

"I think I will stay here tomorrow," said Truthful thoughtfully to Charles, who was seated at her side. Major Harnett was perusing the bookshelves, and the three Newington-Lacys were arguing the merits of racing curricles, messenger pigeons, and steam locomotives in delivering messages and freight.

"Really?" asked Charles. He hesitated, then said, "I did not wish to ask you to do so, but it had occurred to me that if Lady Plathenden intends to use the Emerald, then she will make an even greater effort to either have you assist her, or ensure you cannot play any part against her."

"That thought had also occurred to me," said Truthful. She shivered, and added, "So I will be sensible and stay out of sight. I am not exactly afraid, but I do remember that bone wand, and how she ordered us drowned. . . ."

"I was afraid," said Charles quietly. "I fear drowning, perhaps more than any other kind of death. I have been in several battles, and half a dozen skirmishes, but I was never so afraid as when I was tied to that bowsprit."

"You never showed it," said Truthful. "I thought you were just angry."

"That is how many men hide their fear," said Charles. "I must look up Commander Boling one day and make more fulsome apologies and offer greater thanks."

"For rescuing us?" asked Truthful.

"Not just that," said Charles. "I had our people keep watch on him, for he was in London for some days. Drunk or sober, he never said a word about you. Not one word, not even a hint about a beautiful young lady on a traitor's ship. Few people are so discreet, and even fewer Naval officers!"

"Drunk or sober?" asked Truthful, thinking of many of her father's parties with his officers. "That is no idle boast."

She fell silent then and gazed at the fire, listening to the familiar chitchat of Edmund, Stephen, and Robert. They had moved on from transportation to boxing, and were heatedly discussing a championship match that had taken place when they were all in short pants and none of them could have seen.

"You are tired," said Charles.

"A little," admitted Truthful. She yawned, covered it with her hand, and forced herself to get up. "I was thinking that by this time tomorrow night it should all be over. We will have the Emerald safe, and I can go home and make my father well."

"You intend to go home?" asked Charles softly.

"Yes," said Truthful. "I must."

"Will you come back for the Season?" asked Charles. "To be presented and all that? To seek a . . . to find a suitable husband?"

"I don't know," said Truthful, not looking him in the eye. "I . . . I don't know."

"Well, first things first," said Charles, bowing over her hand. "We must defeat Lady Plathenden, and secure the Emerald. Good night, Newt. Sleep well."

21

THE MASQUERADE BALL

The day of the Masquerade Ball dawned very bright, the weather promising a perfect spring day. Very few of Lord and Lady Otterbrook's guests saw the actual dawn, but Truthful was one of them. She had awoken with the first rays of the sun, and half asleep had called out, "Agatha!" as she had done so many times before, to ask for her chocolate to be brought up.

Having uttered that name there was no more sleep to be had. Truthful slipped from her bed and, though she was not as a rule particularly religious or a great churchgoer beyond every second or third Sunday, she found herself kneeling by her bed and offering up a prayer for Agatha's soul and for her own. She was uncertain on the theology of whether someone of fay parentage actually had a soul, but thought it better to err on the side of caution.

Thinking of caution, she afterward prayed for Charles as well, that he be safe, and then she went through her cousins, and her great-aunt, and the Otterbrooks, and even Sergeant Ruggins, so that by the time she finished it was considerably later and she had very sore knees.

After hot chocolate brought by a maid whose mumbled name was either Maude or Mary, Truthful bathed and dressed, far more carefully than she had for many days. But when at last she went down to breakfast in the most charming dress of Italian crape lined with exquisite Flemish lace, that effort proved to have been wasted. Her intended audience, Charles Otterbrook, had already breakfasted and left the house to supervise a cordon around the Old Ship and to have the Assembly Rooms searched to be sure no infernal devices had been secreted there.

True to her word, and once again erring on the side of caution, Truthful did not leave the house that day. She saw Charles once, when he returned to see that she was still safe and to confer with Sergeant Ruggins, and she saw her cousins several times, severally and together, as they returned for fortifying drinks and snacks and even a hasty luncheon.

As the day dragged on, the tension inside Truthful grew. She began to prowl restlessly about the house until Lady Badgery emerged with fez on head and insisted that they play cards until it was time to begin their preparations for the Masquerade Ball.

Being in Brighton, the ball started early, at eight o'clock. Truthful, Lady Badgery, and Lady Otterbrook took supper together at six. They spoke little, and Truthful spilled her wine. She was glad when it was over and they could go up to dress.

Coming back down shortly before half past seven, she saw Charles already below so she paused on the stair. This time, she caught the light perfectly, the red-gold rays of the setting sun making her white and silver costume flash and her red hair look as if it too were aflame.

Charles looked up and caught his breath, shading his eyes as if blinded by an actual goddess. As he was in costume as Hermes, clad in a golden raiment with wings on his boots, this looked rather theatrical and made Truthful laugh.

"You are a radiant Diana," said Charles. "Have you tested your bow?"

"Thank you, sir," replied Truthful, with a curtsy. She thought he looked very handsome too, but didn't like to say so. "As for the bow, I have put several holes in the wall at the end of the corridor opposite my room. It shoots well enough and the arrows have actual points. Great-aunt's Turkish knife is in my quiver as well, and I am wearing your bracelet."

"Aunt Lucy's bracelet, in fact," said Charles. "She was kind enough to lend it to me."

"Oh," said Truthful. "I wish I had known! I must thank her."

"She will be down soon, I am sure," said Charles. "Aunt Lucy is never late, and she must be first to greet the guests. Though Uncle is already there, practicing with his waves."

"Has there been any sign of Lady Plathenden?" asked Truthful.

"Not yet. Sir Everard is looking through all the guests as they arrive, piercing their glamours and costumery so she shall not get in unobserved. Ah, here are Aunt Lucy and Lady Badgery. A pirate and a . . . I am not entirely sure . . ."

"I am the Empress Theodosia," sniffed Lady Otterbrook, who was wearing a white toga with a purple stripe and a crenelated crown of gold set with large square gems. "I thought anyone could see that."

"It was on the tip of my tongue," said Charles. "Forgive me! You make a very grand empress, Aunt. And a very bold pirate, Lady Badgery. Is that a real cutlass?"

"It is," replied Lady Badgery. "And I had it sharpened

this morning. Holds an edge like a razor, my boy. Like a razor!"

"We had best be getting along," said Charles. "The carriage is ready."

Though it was a very short distance to the Old Ship, it took some time to get there. The crush was not so great as for Lady Mournbeck's ball, many of the guests choosing to walk, but there was an added delay due to the enthusiasm of the constables, who insisted on examining the interior of all conveyances, and they had already arrested three mermaids who proved to be blameless.

However, shortly before eight, Truthful, Charles, and the two elderly ladies were climbing the stair to the Assembly Rooms, past the standing footmen attired as Vikings, most of whom were actually government agents.

"Those axes look surprisingly authentic," whispered Truthful to Charles as they passed through the double doors into the main ballroom, under the musicians' gallery.

"They are," said Charles. "Borrowed them from the Tower, General Leye brought them down this afternoon."

"Charles," called out Lady Otterbrook, "go and fetch your uncle from his ridiculous corner. I need him to stand with me to greet the guests."

"Remember, I should like to dance with you, regardless of our official duties," said Charles, relinquishing

Truthful's arm before heading over to the far corner, where the Marquis, playing the part of King Canute in a horned helmet and a bearskin, was standing on his throne and gesturing at several footmen who had large pasteboard waves affixed to their backs. They were crouched down in a line, and on his signal, slowly shuffled forward and back.

"Lady Truthful, it is a pleasure to see you again."

Truthful turned and smiled at General Leye. He wore the white robe of an ancient druid, complete with a very sharp-looking silvered sickle thrust through his belt of enameled green leaves.

"And you, sir. You know my great-aunt, Lady Badgery?"

"Know him?" whispered Lady Badgery in Truthful's ear. "We were subalterns together in the Buffs."

"What's that you're saying?" inquired General Leye with a twinkle in his eye. "Blackening my name, Ermintrude? I don't suppose you'd care for a rubber or two of piquet?"

"I certainly would, General," replied Lady Badgery. She looked over the ballroom. It was beginning to fill up with gorgeously costumed guests, the orchestra had begun to play, and soon there would be dancing. There was no immediate sign of a malevolent mermaid or Lady Plathenden in any other garb. "Presuming we can be spared. The card tables are in the other chamber, I perceive, as usual?"

"I believe young Otterbrook has matters in hand," said

the general. "In any case, someone must watch in the card-room as well. A shilling a point?"

"Let us say sixpence," replied Lady Badgery, taking his arm. "And a guinea the rubber."

As soon as they had departed, Truthful was once again besieged by gentlemen hopeful to secure a dance. But to every inquiry she gave the same answer, "I am sorry, my ankle is a little strained, I may only dance once tonight, and that dance is spoken for by Lord Lytchett."

Before long this response was noted unfavorably not only by the gentlemen concerned, but by several mothers of the type found terrifying by Edmund Newington-Lacy. They discovered common cause in quietly disparaging comments about Truthful's character, conduct, and dress and in the fact their own offspring had failed to attract Charles Otterbrook's attention at all. They ascribed his apparent penchant for Truthful's company not to her beauty or address, but as likely being due to the viscount—never known as a gamester—suffering some secret loss requiring him to repair his fortune by marrying an heiress.

As the first dances formed up, Truthful wandered about the room, keenly looking at the several mermaids present and anyone else who might be Lady Plathenden. Charles was busy assisting the Marquis, or rather in encouraging him to leave his throne and his waves to join his wife in greeting the guests. Then he walked along the receiving line and took part in what was hoped to be surreptitious conferences with various Viking footmen. But he returned to Truthful as the first waltz was called, and took her in his arms when the music began. They danced in silence for the first few bars, Truthful counting her steps until she relaxed in the knowledge that she did know the dance, and Charles would successfully lead her anyway.

"Any sign?" she asked softly as they twirled near the deserted throne of Canute.

"No," replied Charles worriedly. "We're up to six mermaids arrested now, but none of them are her. It may be as well she doesn't turn up after all. Sir Everard says the Emerald is definitely Canute's *Valdbjarg*. Or rather, his wife Aelfgifu's *Valdbjarg*."

"What does that mean?" asked Truthful.

"Sir Everard says the closest he can make it is 'powerstone,'" said Charles. He was looking over her head, eyes flickering about the crowd. "Which does not sound at all as if the only thing it can do is make or quell storms."

As he spoke, the music suddenly faltered with the shriek of a violin bowed wrong. Charles instantly swung Truthful to the wall and they turned together to look up at the musicians' gallery.

A tall, striking-looking *man* in the ordinary rather drab

evening clothes of a working musician let his violin fall, stood up from the seated musicians, and moved to the railing of the gallery. The conductor there gestured violently with his baton.

"You! Take your seat at—"

He never finished. The tall man plucked open his coat and tore away his neckcloth, and the ballroom was suddenly filled with an eldritch green light that emanated from the brilliant emerald he wore on a silver chain about his throat.

As the light spread, the air swirled in the room, invisible wafts gripping at arms and legs. All movement stopped. Truthful felt the power that came with the air grip her every muscle. Her hand, already to her shoulder, reaching for an arrow, was held motionless. She saw Charles's fingers caught at the opening in his tunic, no doubt reaching for a pocket pistol he could not remove or point.

"Welcome to *my* Masquerade!" declaimed the man, but it was not a male voice. It was higher and piercing: the cold, heartless voice of Lady Amelia Plathenden. "Do not fret! I shall not keep you long. And when we go, we shall all go together. Yes, all of you, who would not grace my parties, who cut me in the street, who would not grant me vouchers to Almack's! Who killed my husband! Even the fat Prince, thinking himself safe in his dwarfish palace. He will go with me too. You will *all* go with me."

A chill breeze followed her words, making the candles flicker in the candelabras high above, and the music on the stands blow off and scatter down like leaves, the only movement in the silent, motionless ballroom.

But it was not the breeze that chilled Truthful's heart. The breeze was only a small harbinger of what Lady Plathenden had truly wrought. Truthful could feel it through her bones, sense it building to the south. For now, it was far off, gathering size and strength. But all too soon it would begin to move.

Lady Plathenden was using the Emerald's power over wind and water to conjure a giant wave.

A wave that would come crashing down upon Brighton. A vast wall of swift water, towering higher than the clouds, it would demolish the grand houses on the Marine Parade, the humble fishermen's cottages to the west, the shops and dwellings in the narrow lanes.

The great wave would smash the Assembly Rooms of the Old Ship to pieces and sweep the Marine Pavilion away, iron framework and all, and the Prince Regent and all his courtiers and guards with it.

As Lady Plathenden said, they would indeed all go together.

Everyone, from the Prince Regent to the humblest fishwife.

All would be killed.

Truthful thought of Charles and his fear of drowning, and resolved that it would not be so. She looked up at Lady Plathenden and saw her outline shiver. In the green light of the Emerald she looked less and less like a man and more like a woman uncomfortably in male clothes. Truthful narrowed her eyes and concentrated on the Emerald.

You should not be doing Lady Plathenden's bidding, Truthful thought fiercely. You should be doing mine! Let me move, for you are my Emerald, as you were my mother's and my grandmother's and so many mothers and grandmothers before them, back to Aelfgifu and beyond. You are mine to command!

"What?" asked Lady Plathenden, apparently to the empty air. She looked down, searching for Truthful. Her head moved from side to side as she gazed into the crowded dance floor, a sea of statues, of popes and kings and queens and gods and goddesses. All masked, disguised, unable to be identified.

Truthful felt a warmth in her fingers, a tingling in her arms, and knew that she could move again. She no sooner felt it than she did move, taking an arrow from her quiver with one swift motion, setting it to her bow, and drawing the bowstring back.

The movement caught Lady Plathenden's attention. She

reached for the bone wand, smoke already trailing from her fingers, a spell begun.

But it was not completed.

Truthful's arrow sped true, sprouting shockingly from Lady Plathenden's eye, the azure fletching no longer the only piece of color, a sudden scarlet spreading down the shaft. The glamour left Plathenden, the bone wand fell from her nerveless hand, and the woman toppled over the railing to crash into the floor below between a unicorn and an unlikely cloth-of-gold-clad milkmaid.

The green light winked out as if it had never been. Truthful ran to the body before anybody else could begin to move. Snatching the Emerald, she broke the silver chain and ran for the door.

"Go to high ground!" she shouted. "She has conjured a giant wave!"

Lady Plathenden might be dead, but the wave lived on. Truthful could feel it, and knew it was moving quickly. It was already more than a hundred feet high and two miles wide, and it would strike the coast in less than fifteen minutes.

She ran down the stairs, jumping three at a time. Startled Vikings clutched their axes and made slow movements as she passed.

"Get everyone to high ground!" shouted Truthful again and again. "High ground!"

Outside, she saw her cousins and the real Major Harnett, but did not pause. They rushed to her, but she did not answer their questions, merely shouting as she ran past them toward the beach.

"High ground! Plathenden called a great wave! Go to high ground!"

It was much darker across the road, away from all the lanterns and flambeaux outside the Old Ship. There were also fishing nets spread out to dry, causing Truthful to stumble and hop and almost fall. She was regaining her balance when a hand steadied her, and she cried out.

"What must you do?" asked Charles tersely. "Get to the sea?"

"Yes!"

"This way, between the nets!"

They ran hand in hand, feet sliding on the pebbles. But the sea was not where it had been, not where Truthful expected. It had drawn back several hundred yards at least, exposing a great expanse of wet pebbly beach, dark in the night.

"Go back, Charles!" she begged. "Run for the hill. Even if I get to the sea in time, I don't know if I can turn the wave!"

Charles did not answer and he didn't let go of her hand. They ran on together, and as they ran, the crescent moon came out from behind a cloud, making the wet beach a silver road.

In the moonlight, they also saw the wave. It looked like a great, dark storm gathering on the horizon, but they both knew better. Splashing and slipping, they threw themselves forward, Truthful casting away the bow that she hadn't even realized she'd still been holding all that time.

At last they plunged into the sea itself, too vigorously, both going under and coming back up spluttering.

"Hold me," ordered Truthful, bracing her feet against the small waves that sought to push her over. Charles stood behind her, leaning forward, his hands around her waist.

Truthful raised the Emerald, looked into it, and bent all her will on turning back the vast wave that filled the sky.

22

COMPLETELY AND THOROUGHLY COMPROMISED

Green light fell from Truthful's fingers, brighter than the moon. The waves that had threatened to bowl her over quieted, and the sea in front of her grew still. Slowly this spread till the crash of surf all but disappeared, replaced by the softest lapping of the sea on stones.

"I can't turn it completely," whispered Truthful. "It is too strong."

Charles's arms tightened around her, and he kissed the top of her left ear.

"Perhaps it is too much to ask that you save my life *three* times," he said softly. "May I say I love you before we drown?"

"I can't turn it," said Truthful, ignoring this remark. "But . . . I have diminished it, I think. . . . What was that?"

"I love you," said Charles. "I just wanted to say it."

"I love you too, idiot," replied Truthful affectionately. She lowered the Emerald, but the green light didn't fade and the immediate sea remained calm. "I think I have done all I can. We don't need to stay here and we certainly don't need to drown."

"What?" exclaimed Charles. He looked across the moonlit sea. There was no longer an awful, horizon-spanning darkness. But there was a very large hump upon the water, a hump that was growing closer by the second.

Truthful looked back up the beach. She vaguely remembered some structure, standing tall, closer than the houses on the Parade. A pump house for the seawater cure, the guidebook had said. . . .

"There!" she shouted, pointing. "Run!"

Running up a pebbly beach was even more difficult than running down it. Both of them fell several times, and each time they got up they could not help looking back. The wave was very close, and the calm and quiet of the sea in front of it was no longer reassuring but had more the air of a horrified silence before some terrible act of violence.

They reached the pump house mere moments before the wave hit. Truthful had hoped to climb it somehow, but all they could do was shelter in its lee. Truthful wrapped both arms and legs around Charles, and Charles gripped the iron handle of the door just as the still enormous wave came crashing down with an earsplitting roar.

———————

Lady Badgery found them there a half hour later, in a puddle of seawater. Charles had his back to the door and Truthful was sitting in his lap. The wave had knocked them about, but not enough to break them free or carry them back into the sea. Thanks to Truthful's efforts to reduce its power, it had generally failed to destroy much of anything, though there were many houses now with cellars full of dirty, salty water.

"So I suppose you are going to marry my great-niece after all," said Lady Badgery. "Or so I hope, she being utterly compromised by your lascivious caresses."

"I am holding on to Lady Truthful in case of further waves," said Charles with all the dignity he could muster, given that he was completely sodden and his golden tunic was ripped in several places. "And we have agreed that we do love one another and will marry as soon as possible."

"Yes," said Truthful. She held up the jewel on its broken silver chain, the soft green light making her own eyes shine. "Look! I have got back the Emerald."

"So you have," said Lady Badgery. "I knew you would.

Now Ned owes me five pounds. He bet against the marriage too, more fool him. But perhaps you should stand up. Here come your cousins."

"Oh, very well," grumbled Charles. They both stood up, but even so Truthful nestled at his side.

Stephen was the first to arrive. He saw the Emerald in Truthful's left hand and laughed, and then laughed again as he saw her right hand was firmly clasped by Charles.

"I knew you could do it, Newt! The Emerald back and a marquis to wed!"

"He's not a marquis," said Truthful. "He's only a viscount."

Charles coughed and bent his head toward his intended.

"In the interest of ensuring you know *everything*," he said, "I am my uncle's heir. One day I will be a marquis."

"You'd best kiss him," said Lady Badgery to Truthful. "While it's still just family. Before Sergeant Ruggins and Major Harnett arrive."

"I will," said Truthful, and did exactly as she said.

AUTHOR'S NOTE

I wrote the first version of this book many years ago, between 1990 and 1991. Back then, it was a book within a book, a thriller set in a publishing house that receives a Regency romance manuscript that contains clues to a criminal conspiracy. As I love both genres, I thought this was a wonderful idea, but the publishers of the time did not share my view. Later, I reluctantly had to agree that while the idea was interesting, my execution of it was not. The two books did not work as one.

Over time, the thriller portion of this combined book became more and more outdated (it was before mobile phones, and a significant plot point involved 3.5-inch floppy disks) and so it remains in a bottom drawer and there it will stay.

However, *Newt's Emerald* did not have such problems, and every now and then I transferred the manuscript to a new computer and read it again and thought about doing something with it. Finally, in 2013, I decided the time had come. I figured it wouldn't be much work, but as per usual, I was wrong. This book is substantially different from that earlier manuscript. It is more than a third longer and departs significantly in terms of plot and character. However, in essence it is still the same story.

As anyone who reads Regency romances knows, the "founding mother" of the genre is Georgette Heyer, and *Newt's Emerald* would never have been written if I had not discovered a cache of her books when I was about thirteen. I also owe a debt to Jane Austen and Patrick O'Brian. All three are favorite authors of mine, and one of the great "research" pleasures I engaged in during the rewriting of this book was to reread all of Heyer's Regency romances, most of Austen, and the entire Aubrey-Maturin series. Again.

These are some of the influences, along with numerous others for the fantasy elements, including those trusty companions myth and legend. Anything good in the book can undoubtedly be put to the account of these influences. Anything less good must be claimed as my own.

I must also thank Kali Ciesemier for the wonderful cover of the original ebook; my agent, Jill Grinberg, and her team; my publisher, Katherine Tegen, and her staff at HarperCollins; and as always, my wife, Anna; my children, Thomas and Edward; and all my family and friends.

—Garth Nix, Sydney, 1991–2014 and Brighton, England, 2013

GLOSSARY

While the world of *Newt's Emerald* departs from the historical in various ways, much is based upon England in the Regency period between 1811 and 1820 when George III was deemed unfit due to his "madness" and his son, the future George IV, ruled. Here are explanations of some of the words used in that period. If I've missed anything particularly puzzling, it is usually easy enough to google; there are many Regency resources on the Internet.

barouche—a four-wheeled carriage
Bow Street Runners—precursors of the London
    metropolitan police, official thieftakers who were
    headquartered in the Bow Street magistrates' offices

flummery—a sweet pudding, but used in slang to mean empty, sugary talk

foxed—drunk

gamester—a gambler

hack or hackney—a (horse-drawn) cab for hire, can also mean an ordinary riding horse

high grig—in good spirits, happy

man-milliner—a male hatmaker, but used in upper-class slang as an expression of contempt for a dandy

on-dit—a rumor or piece of gossip

piquet—a card game

post chaise—a closed traveling carriage, usually drawn by four horses, "a coach and four"

pot valiant—brave due to drink, like "Dutch courage"

rack up—to sleep somewhere

remittance man—someone sent funds by their family from overseas, often to stay away from home due to their bad reputation

sgian dubh—a Scottish knife, usually worn with traditional Highland dress

slow-top—an idiot

The Hundred Days—in real history, the period between Napoleon Bonaparte's return from exile on Elba and his ultimate defeat at Waterloo, the reestablishment of King Louis XVIII and Napoleon's exile to Saint

Helena. In this book, Napoleon is a bit different and is imprisoned by magic within the Rock of Gibraltar.

tiger—a boy groom, fashionable in this period. They often wore striped livery, hence the name.

ton—a term meaning the most fashionable and high-status members of British society in this period

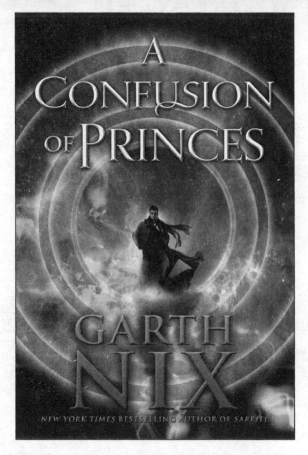